About the Author

Morgan Mei lives in Australia, on the land of the Gadigal people of the Eora Nation. She has also lived in London, Munich, a travelling circus, and the worlds of many books. *Also, I Love You* is Morgan's first novel.

Also, I Love You

Morgan Mei

Also, I Love You

Olympia Publishers
London

www.olympiapublishers.com
OLYMPIA PAPERBACK EDITION

A CIP catalogue record for this title is
available from the British Library.

ISBN: 978-1-80439-108-2

First Published in 2023

**Olympia Publishers
Tallis House
2 Tallis Street
London
EC4Y 0AB**

Printed in Great Britain

Dedication

For Catriona, whom I love to such tiny pieces.

Acknowledgements

My effusive and heartfelt thanks to my incredible, patient, and very beloved beta reading team: Claire, one of my oldest and dearest friends, without whom this book would never exist. I really thought I was done with writing until Holly, and I wrote this while waiting my turn. You've always looked out for me; you're just amazing and I love you. Brody, who put the most time and effort into notes for this story, read fast so I wouldn't get anxious, and took me on motorbike rides when I needed breaks from life. You're my family and you're grape. Kate, who is this book's biggest fan – I will forever love you for that (and other reasons too numerous to list). You deserve the whole world, lady. Also to my sweet friends – Liz, whom I met in Inappropriate Circumstances and is a constant source of inspiration and joy. Kim, who's been my cheerleader in life in general and who talked me into this publishing thing. My favourite authors, because I'm pretty sure I just patch-worked their writing styles to make my own, so to Markus Zusak, Holly Black, Catherynne M. Valente, Sally Thorne, and Nick Harkaway – thank you for making escape hatches. And to anyone who is reading this book – you are making my dreams come true. Thank you so much, I hope it makes you feel warm and fuzzy inside.

One

Repanthe

THE WIND gusted a slew of raindrops down Raven's collar, and set her teeth to chattering. She gasped at the sensation, but grinned while tugging her scarf up around her chin. It always seemed odd to others, but Raven loved cold weather best. Especially when she was seconds away from her own front door, and the glowing heart of her house.

She touched the ivy and rowan wreath on her door, and stepped inside. Her coat and boots came off in a hurry before she crossed the room, spun on the spot and dropped heavily onto the hearth rug. Raven sighed. The warmth of the fire was divine on her back, and she spread her rain-heavy wings to its heat.

A low chuckle issued from the staircase at the side of the room.

"You're dripping on the carpet," Arden said.

Raven groaned and leaned over her out-stretched legs. She moved her wings slowly back and forth, their filmy surface refracting orange light across the floor like so much spilled egg yolk. The smoke still smelled like sage.

"It's my carpet to drip on," Raven retorted, closing her eyes. "That's kind of the point."

Arden sat down opposite her, and handed over a towel.

"Did you get everything on your list?" he asked her.

"I think so," Raven replied. She dragged the towel over her

face, and squeezed out her hair. "It's hard to tell at this point. I've never set up my own home before."

"Well, as first own homes go, I think this is lovely."

Raven had to agree. It had been a just week since she had packed up and moved out to the city, and her house was small but perfect. It was the skinny half of a run-down townhouse. The ground level had a tiny kitchenette to the right of the doorway, and then, beyond, a snug sitting room with a fireplace. On the left-hand wall, a narrow staircase led up and around to the bedroom on one side and the bathroom on the other. It was just enough room for one, but still it seemed that every day she was discovering things that she hadn't realised she needed. First, it was an armchair for the sitting room. Obvious. Then, a kettle and toaster, which had been supplied when she lived at the lake house. A laundry hamper. A bath mat. Today she had gone and picked out a set of wine glasses and some large mixing bowls, and she thought surely, now she had everything. Which, unfortunately, meant she was losing the thing that mattered the most.

"Do you really have to go?" Raven put the damp towel in her lap and looked up at Arden's scruffy face. He sighed, the liquid onyx eyes of his oldest friend wide and playing innocent. Usually, that worked on him.

"I really do, kid," he said. "One week. That was the deal."

Raven had been planning this, her big venture into the real world, for a month. After high school, she, Arden and a couple of their friends had rented a run-down house from an old selkie, and lived next to the lake for a few years. But lately it had seemed to Raven that that didn't really count as independence. In the house by the lake, she had learned to cook for herself, completed an undergrad degree, and lost her virginity to a shape-shifter, who had, disconcertingly, flitted through fifteen different faces as he finished.

But now Raven was looking for the next step. After all, she was still living in her small fae hometown, with friends she'd known since childhood. Their landlady took care of the administration and maintenance of running a home, and her parents weren't far if she ever really ran into trouble. So, the week before her twenty-first birthday, Raven applied for a further studies programme at Repanthe University, and was accepted almost immediately. They had come under fire in the media recently for lack of diversity, and a well-performing fae student was just what their image needed. They had even offered to place her with student accommodation, a low-cost option that meant Raven could live on her own and still afford rent.

Now that she was actually here, in her own inner-city dwelling, with Arden due to leave any moment, the fear began to sink in. It congealed thick in her gut. Raven shuffled closer, knees of their crossed legs knocking together, and reached up to cup her hands around Arden's pointed, wolf ears. The soft fur blended smoothly into the thick of his hair, and she rubbed the base of his ears just like he liked. Arden's yellow eyes fluttered closed in pleasure.

"What about just one more night?" she whispered. He laughed softly in his throat, without opening his eyes.

"I suppose it *is* pretty horrendous weather for travel." He leaned forward into Raven's hands.

"What about just one more week?"

Arden just snorted in response, and pulled away. Raven had expected as much. She wanted to find independence, and put herself in the big wide world. But life without Arden? In such a close-knit community, all the children had grown up together and looked after each other. But Arden and Raven were born on the same day, their mothers were best friends, and they were inseparable. Especially after Arden's father died, and Arden started spending more time with Raven's family than his own. Everyone called them 'the twins', much to their delight, and when they were faelings, they had pretended they really did have matching DNA.

"Repanthe is no place for me," Arden said. "It stinks of iron, and I'd never fit in."

"And I would?" Raven retorted.

"You look like them but prettier," Arden said, tugging the end of one of her wings. "I'm too big, too *scary*."

Arden was wolfkin – looked human from the waist up, with the exception of his ears. But around his hips, his russet skin gave way to tawny fur. His tail was usually tucked up against his back, although it tended to flick back and forth when he was upset. And from the knees down, his shins melted into great, grey, wolf legs. Arden often wore long trousers but his giant, clawed feet were always bare. The thick pads didn't need the protection of shoes, and the expense of custom-made boots didn't seem worth it just to fit in on rare city trips.

Raven, on the other hand, looked more human – at least from the front. She was small and slender, with milky skin, delicate features and tumbling blue-black hair, for which her mother had named her. Her eyes, too, were completely black, with the same inhuman glow that Arden had, and her ears pulled into tips at the top. And then of course there were the large, iridescent wings sprouting from her back. But Arden was right; faeries generally had a much easier time in the city than any of the chimera Folk. The more human you looked, the less harassment you got.

"You're pretty too," Raven mumbled.

Truthfully, though, they knew it would probably do them so good to spend time apart. Their mothers always said so, said as they got older, they needed to grow their own personalities and not be so co-dependent. And while she loved Arden, Raven did want to know that she was capable of living life without leaning on him all time. She had a fear deep down that there was something un-feminist about relying on a man, that she was supposed to know who she was and what she wanted by herself.

And, finally, there was The Incident, that they had not discussed and were both successfully ignoring. They each privately figured that if they pretended it didn't happen long enough, that would be true.

"Just one more night," Arden said. He lifted his big shaggy head, and wrinkled his nose.

"Now go take a shower," he said. "You smell like iron already."

Under the soft, down duvet, Raven stared at the ceiling and listened to the dull rhythm of the rain. Beneath it, Arden's quiet snore climbed up to reach her, from where his hefty frame was sprawled out on the carpet. Arden hadn't complained at all about sleeping on the floor all week, and even though she couldn't see him from the bed, his presence was as solid and comforting as her heavy blankets. He was still home to her, and Raven tried hard to imprint the memories onto her brain to tide her over until she could see them at Yuletide:

The pine trees, making up most of the dense forest surrounding their hometown of Cressock and giving it its signature smell. The salt lake that everyone flocked to every summer, and by which Raven and Arden had lived in their first years out of home. The rows of shops around the town square —

baker, butcher, tailor (bespoke tailoring was a must in fae towns, of course. Raven's clothes, for example, usually had openings for her wings). Library, woodworker, doctor, candy maker (still Arden's favourite place in town). The high school, with its gothic facades and arcing ceilings high enough for you to stretch your wings in. Mountains you could get lost in over the weekend. Arden's lovely face; his rumbling growl; and laughing, yellow eyes.

The next morning seeped through the window, despite Raven's best efforts to prevent it. It wasn't at all apologetic, just clear and sunny as if it weren't here to take Arden away. Raven held on to him around the waist, and generally got under his feet while he packed up the few things he had brought with him when he was helping her move. His old pick-up truck looked much bigger when he threw his bag in the back, now empty of all of Raven's belongings. Now there was not much to be done, but get on the road and drive the six hours back to Cressock.

"Don't look at me like that," Arden said. She folded her arms tightly over her chest and tried for a smile. Arden barked out a laugh.

"Okay, that's much worse."

Raven abandoned the attempt, and Arden sighed.

"Come here, you big baby." He folded his arms around her small shoulders. "You're going to be just fine. Nothing will be as good without you, of course, but I promise you'll be okay."

Raven buried her face in his chest, and asked the question she was holding in the depths of her heart to his shirt. "Am I making a huge mistake?"

Arden pushed her back and tilted her chin up with the crook of his finger. "Raven Lightfoot, you are my best friend in the whole world and you know I don't want you to leave me. But I also know that if you don't do this thing, you'd just be restless and bored at home, and you'll always wonder what's out there. You've got this, Lightfoot."

Raven just nodded, and crushed herself into his chest one more time.

"I'll call you when I get home," Arden said gently.

"Nothing will be as good without you, either," Raven said.

"Well, that's a given."

And just like that, Arden was gone, and further away from Raven than he had ever been in their whole lives.

Raven spent the rest of the day pottering about the house, putting away her most recent purchases and settling her things just so. It felt good to spend time on her house, like she was pulling it a little tighter around herself and fitting it snugly to her. She had never lived alone, and the prospect was certainly daunting, but she did have the advantage of her being able to organise everything exactly as she wanted. This would be her safe haven in the big concrete-and-iron city. Classes started up tomorrow, and Raven felt as prepared as she could be. In the last few hours of the day, she decided to take a walk.

She stepped out and took a deep breath, turning her head to get her bearings. The smell of old rust scratched faintly at Raven's throat, and the crisp air tripped its fingers over her cheekbones. Either side of her, rectangular buildings rose up stoically from the pavement. They were a melting pot of the old cities in the Human Realm, and nothing seemed to match. Raven turned right, and walked towards the city centre.

In the dimming twilight, the sky grew darker but no stars came out. The lights from the buildings seemed to dazzle in their place, and Raven supposed these were beautiful, too. She had been out and about a little with Arden over the past week, but they concentrated on getting the house ready, finding the best route to the university, and picking up the things she would need for her classes. But now she had her eye out for more affordable shops, for grocery stores, for places she might like to come eat some time. She attracted a few odd looks as she walked, but that was normal.

Repanthe had the highest human population in the Realm, and fae were thin on the ground here. It was the first city to be settled and colonised after the Realm War two hundred years ago, and hallmarks of occupation still remained: the human faces on the currency, their rounded ears in plain sight on the likenesses in profile. The scent of iron in the air from purpose-built walls. The scanners over doorways, now well out of use, of course, that used to check for non-human features before entry to swanky clubs. Although Repanthe had long outlawed such discriminating practices, it was well known that the clothing stores generally stocked human only, and bespoke tailors were harder to find and much more expensive here. Besides, fae memories were long, and two hundred years was within some Folk's living recollection. Not a popular choice for settling fae families, then.

Repanthe was the biggest city in the realm, and, years and centuries ago, the home of the Seelie Court. Of course, the courts were razed to the ground during the occupation, but Repanthe, with paved roads reaching out like arms in every direction that mattered, was quickly resettled. The other major attraction of Repanthe was the large inland harbour, which connected all the way out to West Bay by a winding canal. Huge trading ships gilded up and down like metal sharks.

The ground under Raven's boots was cobblestoned along the

footpath, but the main roads were dug out and tarred over in the rebuilding of the city. Blackened rainwater tricked through the gutters that bordered them, catching on the occasional coffee cup or cigarette butt. It seemed that everything here was coloured grey. Even the Folk – *people*, Raven corrected herself – in their charcoal overcoats and creased brows, seemed to walk with concrete bones. The closer Raven got to the city centre, the taller the buildings grew. She stared up and around, in a forest of glass and steel, until someone jostled her from behind and reminded her you weren't supposed to just stop in the street. Raven walked quickly on.

Eventually, Raven hit a social-looking area, where fingers of music wafted through the air. She ducked into a pub with a green door. That always meant luck, to her. The sign said *The Rainbow Connection,* and inside it was small and dimly lit. There was a neon sign behind the bar that cast an eerie glow across the whole room. The bartender was a heavyset human man with a tea towel thrown over one shoulder, who was writing on the blackboard on the wall, and didn't seem to notice her.

A few places down from her, Raven found a menu – a scuffed, laminated affair with bar snacks on one side and drinks on the other. Lots of house-made beers, a human specialty. A few locally sourced fae wines, very expensive. Absinthe that probably wasn't real, not by faerie standards anyway.

"The gin's good."

Raven turned at the voice, and found a handsome human man smiling at her a few places down the bar. She smiled back hesitantly. In the country, you could make conversation with anyone. In the city, wasn't she not supposed to talk to strangers?

"I've never had gin."

At least, that's the rule they gave to faelings.

"No?" he responded. "Would you let me order you one?"

And yet what an absolute thrill that an attractive male was trying to buy her a drink. Raven tried not to blush like a school girl, took a breath and said, "Sure."

The young man got up and moved down next to her. She caught a whiff of his cologne, and found it surprisingly pleasant. Citrus and sandalwood.

"Two G&Ts. Hendrick's," he said, tapping his fingers on the bar to get the other man's attention. He turned back to Raven. "It's Elias, by the way."

"Raven." She shook his hand. Her heart beat a little faster, and she reasoned with herself that she had to meet people *somehow*.

Elias had sandy hair, a fashionably short beard, and friendly eyes. A couple of years older than her, judging by the crinkle of his smile and how easy this interaction seemed to be for him. Raven crossed her ankles under the bar stool. New people always made her nervous, especially humans. She pulled her wings in a little tighter, as the bar tended put two short glasses down in front of them. He took Elias' card, and managed the whole interaction without looking at Raven at all.

"So, Raven. I haven't seen you around here before. Trying out a new pub?"

"Sort of. Actually, all the pubs are new to me. I just moved here." She slid her fingers over the cold glass.

"Oh, my condolences. Welcome, it's disgusting here." Elias grinned, and raised his drink.

"Thanks. I'm just excited to be living in the city, finally."

"Where are you from?" He leaned in closer to her, and she tried to relax her shoulders.

"Little town called Cressock?"

"Never heard of it." That didn't surprise her. "Cheers."

They clinked glasses together, and Raven took a sip. It was cold and refreshing, sweet but not overwhelming, and the juniper made her feel nostalgic.

"It's, uh, about six hours drive from here. It's pretty lovely, actually."

"Oh yeah? Tell me about it."

"Well, uh, it's surrounded by forest so the air smells like pine. You can pick mushrooms the size of dinner plates. And we have the best pies in the world." Raven let out a nervous laugh. "Do I sound like a complete country bumpkin?"

Elias shook his head. "No, you sound utterly adorable. I'm sure it's just gorgeous."

Raven looked down at her hands. "So, ah, where did you grow up?"

"Right here. I'm a Repanthe man through and through, I'm afraid. I hope you won't hold it against me." Elias took a sip of his drink.

"Do you really hate it that much?" Raven asked. He smiled.

"Of course not. Don't listen to me. As a general rule."

"Right, so then I won't ask you what's good to do around here."

Elias scoffed. "Well, not this bar for starters. It's a dump, I just come here out of habit. But, in all honesty, most of the rumours about the city are true: the food's great, there's always people awake, and the music scene will move you. You're going to love it." He tipped his head to the side. "You ever see the harbour at night time?" Raven shook her head. Elias flashed a white-toothed grin.

"Got anywhere to be tonight?"

Raven paused. Okay *this* she definitely should not do. Axe

murders, dark alleys, etc, etc.

"Nowhere at all."

Elias walked her down by the dock, and the smell of iron was particularly strong in the harbour. Raven didn't mention it; it wasn't something she expected humans to remember. She tried to put it out of her mind, and focus on the massive ships, bobbing silently around her.

"Come on," Elias said. He took her hand, the foreign touch startling her a little. Raven tried not to let it show.

Elias led her past the boats and to a low bench overlooking the water, and slung his arms over the back of the bench once they were seated. Across the harbour, the city stood tall and proud. Below, reflected lights danced merrily with the little waves that lapped at the docks.

"This is my favourite spot in the city," Elias said. "You still feel like you're in the middle of it all, but it's quieter out here and you're not about to get run over at any given moment."

"It's beautiful," Raven said.

They sat for a while longer, while Elias told her things about city life. She reckoned by the glint in his eye about half of them were entirely made-up, and outright laughed at him when he told her it was customary for city people to enter a room backward the first time they came in.

"It's true!" Elias protested. "Going backwards is respectful, because it shows you're willing to be vulnerable to your host."

"That is absolutely not true," Raven giggled. "Just because fae can't lie doesn't mean we don't know when someone else is."

"Okay, okay." Elias put his hands up. "I made that one up. But the one about the frogs is real."

"I'm ignoring you now."

"At your own peril."

"I accept the risks."

Elias chuckled his defeat.

"All right, you win. I should ask you for embarrassing secrets, as a consolation prize. Since you can't lie."

Raven leaned back, finding herself more and more at ease with the stranger.

"Sure, I can't lie, but I also don't have to tell you the truth."

Elias cocked his head to one side. "Am I the most handsome human man you've ever met?"

In actual fact, he was. How outrageous that he knew it. Raven looked him straight in the eye.

"You're the *only* human man I've ever known, so I could also tell you you're the most vile and it'd be equally true." Known, not met. She'd never had a conversation this long with a human before. Elias laughed delightedly.

"All right, tricksy faerie. It's getting late, why don't you let me walk you home?"

Raven agreed, and they strolled back to the townhouse. Elias tucked her arm in his, and put his jacket over her shoulders when she shivered, just like in the movies.

Luckily, he was big enough that the jacket went right over her wings.

It was late enough that the streets were no longer crowded, but the background roar of traffic was apparently a constant in the city. It crossed Raven's mind that all things considered, her little house actually had quite good sound-proofing.

"So, this is me."

"You live here?" Elias asked. "You're such a student."

Raven laughed. "What does that mean?"

"It means all the hip, young, penniless students live in this area. Who knew you'd be such a cliché for an out-of-towner?"

Raven bumped him with her shoulder. "Hey, don't blame me, I didn't know any better."

"Well, we'll have to see if we can't get you educated."

They stopped at Raven's front door, and Elias pulled out his phone, tipping it towards her.

"First two lessons are free if you sign up now. This is the part where you give me your number, by the way."

Raven laughed. "Are you sure?" she teased.

"I'm sure." Elias gave a cocky grin that was almost enough for her to deny him out of spite.

Almost.

Raved bit her lip, and took the phone. Once her number was saved, Elias slipped it back into his pocket and kissed her on the cheek.

"Lovely to meet you, Raven." He winked. "I'll talk to you soon."

After he had gone, Raven let herself in and grinned as she peeled off and hung up her layers. She rushed into the bedroom and switched the heater on. Then she hurried to the bathroom and got the hot water going. Without Arden around to light the fire before she got back, the house was freezing. She turned her face up to the water, and let it thaw her out. Another wonderful, wintry kind of feeling. And here it was only autumn.

While the water warmed her bones, Raven hugged herself and thought about her number in Elias' pocket. It made her feel that her first night on her own was a wild success, and her ego was enjoying the boost.

And if it was completely dumb to give her number to a man she'd just met? Then she was out on her own, and there was no one to judge her anyway, dumb decision or no, and wasn't that marvellous?

Stepping out of shower, Raven wrapped herself in a towel and padded to the now toasty bedroom. She went to close the door, and then remembered again. For the first time in her life, she was in this house alone. Raven grinned, and then dropped the towel. She giggled, still half expecting someone to walk in and humiliate her. But of course, no one did. She walked back to the bathroom, nude, then to the bedroom. Back and forth down the hall a couple of times, before she got cold again and shut the bedroom door. She shook off her wings, and flopped down on the bed. The cotton was smooth and cool on her bare skin. For all that she had loved share-housing with her old school friends, this was such a pleasure.

Raven wriggled down between her sheets. She picked up her phone, and there was a missed call from Arden. There was also a text from an unknown number that she assumed was Elias.

Lovely evening with you, it read. *Does this make me your first friend in the city?*

I guess it does, she wrote back. *Thanks for showing me around.*

Oh, I'm not nearly done. I'm writing the itinerary for the next tour as we speak. Clear your schedule Friday night, I've got plans for us...

Raven smiled.

Goodnight, Elias.

Goodnight, Raven.

Raven settled back, feeling heavy, and warm, and content. She hit the contact for Arden, and sniffed the pillow he had been using for any remainder of the smell of him as the phone rang.

"Hello?" came Arden's voice, thick with sleep.

"Oh sorry, did I wake you?"

"Mmm, s'okay, I always want to talk to you. How was your first day solo?"

Raven grinned and slid further down in bed.

"Really good, I think. I've been working on the house, and I made a friend already."

"Oh yeah?" Arden yawned, and Raven could picture him propping himself up against the headboard. "That's good stuff. How did you end up doing the lounge room, did you put the photos up?"

"Yes, that one of us in the snow is my absolute favourite."

They chatted about Raven's house for the next half hour, until Arden couldn't stay awake any more. They never did get around to Raven's new friend.

The next day was Raven's first class. She double-checked the contents of her satchel, pulled her beanie on, and set off for the university. One of the major perks of student housing was proximity to the school, which itself was in the heart of Repanthe. The walk was only supposed to be fifteen minutes, but five minutes in, she had slowed down to crawling pace. It seemed that the entire student body walked this way, and a river of young people oozed thickly down the road with her. Elias had been right. Raven dodged around a few students, trying to keep up a brisk walking pace. She looked up at the sky, wondering if maybe she should just fly. But Arden's misgivings about fitting in in a largely human university were fresh in her memory. Also, there were heavy, black cables crisscrossing the street above their heads – telephone wires that in most towns were laid underground. But here they towered over her, effectively making sure she had a ceiling at all times. Repanthe was not doing her any favours.

When they reached the university, the road opened up and the crowd of students dispersed a little, as they all headed off in various directions of their respective classes. Raven breathed a little easier, and consulted her timetable and a large map display. The main building loomed over them, more stainless steel and glass. Nothing at all like the crumbling old buildings in Cressock. The Arts faculty was on the far side of campus, and after being relegated to snail's pace on the way there, Raven had to hurry to arrive on time. She found the right building, and walked through the arches to a stony quadrangle. This looked more like what she was used to – no glass walls in sight. Dry, browned leaves blew around her feet, and in the shadows it was even colder than it had been on the walk here. She quickly located the tutorial room, and slid into a seat near the back.

Raven's undergrad major had been sociology. She was now in a post grad certificate on trauma psychology, and as she looked around the room, she saw they were all around her age or older. And almost all of them seemed to be human. Certainly, the lecturer was human, a middle-aged, white man with mousy hair and horn-rimmed glasses. She wondered if he had any personal experience with trauma, although it was hard to imagine that this soft-bellied man had too many skeletons in his closet. She looked around the room again. There was a tree nymph seated in the second row, and Raven felt slightly more at ease. She focused on taking down notes from the lecture.

"We know that adverse childhood events have significant impact on a person's adult attachment styles and overall wellbeing, including mental and indeed physical health outcomes," the lecturer was saying. "Anything from parents' messy divorce to childhood sexual abuse can have lasting effects on one's psyche. Socioeconomic factors play a role here, too.

Certain groups are more likely to have experienced trauma in their life, among these, people from a lower socioeconomic background, people with disabilities, the Fair Folk, and so on.

"With that said, I hope that hope that in this class we can find more about what binds us together, than what separates us. In order to get to know each other, please walk around the room and find at least two people you have things in common with."

Raven headed down towards the nymph girl. It wasn't very creative, but she also wasn't going to make an elephant in the room about it. The nymph turned as Raven approached, and grinned.

"Let me guess," she said. "You think we might both have January birthdays."

"Damn," said Raven. "Mine's September."

"Oh, soon?"

"Just gone."

"How old?"

"Twenty-one."

"Aww little baby. I'll be twenty-nine next year." The nymph girl pulled a face. "One year before thirty."

Raven laughed. "Nymphs live to two hundred years old, what are you complaining about?"

"You're right, you're right. But do you know my aunt started getting brown spots at fifty?" She extended a slender, pale green hand. "I'm Nola."

"Raven."

Nola, like most tree nymphs, would start out with fresh green skin, and get darker as she aged, until she was a brown, papery old lady. She had twisting, ropey hair, dark green vines and tendrils, with little white flowers sprouting here and there. She wore a loose shift dress, gold bangles on her wrists, and a series of tiny gold hoops in her pointed ears.

"Are you new here, Raven?"

"Yeah, how did you know?"

Nola laughed. "You made a bee-line for the only other fae in the room. How long have you been in Repanthe?"

"One week?"

"Oh, precious thing! Okay, give me your phone. Now, Repanthe can be pretty unforgiving, but don't give up on this place. It needs more fae. I'll show you the places you need to know to get by." Raven was surprised by Nola's instant hospitality, and had to admit she felt a sense of relief.

"That's very kind of you. I noticed it's pretty... human-centric." Raven took her phone back, quietly satisfied at now having two friends in the city. Nola laughed.

"You really are new. It's okay, we still have fae shops, you just need to know where to look."

"Thanks."

"Of course."

At that moment, a human student sat down on Raven's other side.

"Hello, ladies," he said, swinging a leg over his chair to sit in it backwards. "Would you like to be my three? What things are we finding in common, favourite colour, favourite movie, general hobbies and interests? Dancing, we all like dancing, yes?"

"Sure," said Nola.

"I like dancing," Raven said.

"Great! Well, that was easy. I'm Dev."

"I'm Nola, and this is Raven."

Dev had warm, brown skin and fancy sneakers. His long, dark eyelashes were balanced out well by his strong eyebrows, and Raven thought he was pretty.

The lecturer called their attention back.

"I hope you are satisfied with your groups," he said, "for they will be your team for the first group assignment."

The whole glass groaned. A group assignment on their first day? Every student's worse nightmare.

"You can find the assignment details in your Unit of Study outline. Please arrange a time to get together before the end of class, and put your names on board so I know what groups you're in."

"Oooh, okay, let's swap socials. Are you guys free Thursday or Friday evening?" Dev pulled out his phone.

"I can't on Thursday, I have an evening shift at the hospital." Nola sat back in her seat.

"I can't Friday, I, uh, have a date?"

Nola stared at Raven. "You've been here a week and you've got a date? Well, I underestimated you, little faeling. Good for you."

"I don't actually know if it's a date. A guy I met at a bar is showing me around the city."

"Oh, that's definitely a date," Dev said. "On my first date with my boyfriend, he said he wanted to 'show me somewhere' and we ended up having sex under a bridge."

"Great, thanks for sharing, Dev." Nola rolled her eyes. "Okay, can you guys do Wednesday?"

They could. And now Raven knew three people in the city.

The rest of the week went by smoothly. Raven got to know Nola and Dev quite quickly, as they had classes every day and started their assignment in the enormous university library. Nola was a part-time nurse at the local hospital, and Dev lived with his parents in a large house on the city outskirts.

Throughout the week, Elias texted her.

Woke up with you on my mind today. Visit me in your sleep?

She bit her lip as she texted back. *Funny, I didn't dream at all.* The reply came back almost instantly.

How terrible. I have a hundred things to show you on Friday, we'll fill that pretty head with things to dream of.

Are you suggesting my head is empty? Raven wrote back.

Not at all, just that your nights will be better with me in them. As the days went by, the flirting only got more brazen.

How did you get that little scar by your ear? He texted one day.

How do you know about that? She could practically hear his low laugh in his text.

I saw it at the bar. It was very difficult not to look at your neck, it's distractingly gorgeous.

Surrounded by her fellow students in the library, Raven felt her face heat.

Creep, she texted back.

But she found herself flattered anyway, and began to feel both nervous and excited in anticipation of his texts.

Raven had no classes on Thursdays, and spent her time looking for a job. She traipsed around the city with resumés in hand before ending up back at the university. The library was hiring, and they took her on, that same day. Her boss was a human, mid-thirties, with a goatee and long brown hair bundled up under a loose beanie. He gave Raven a few tasks to get started with, and then left her alone the rest of the day. This suited her just fine. The library was magnificent, with innumerable rows of books in the stacks and a large, open study space. The back wall had a huge stained-glass window, throwing colours haphazardly over the desks. Raven was more than happy to be spending extended hours in here. It smelled of old books and wood, and not at all of iron.

On Friday, Elias cancelled.

I'm so sorry, the text read. *Just can't get away from work. Can we do next week? I'll make it up to you.*

Next week is fine by me, Raven texted back.

But suddenly without plans, Raven faced her first weekend properly alone. No housemates, no date, just her and her four walls. She slept in, made a more elaborate breakfast than she usually would, and ate it in front an upbeat sitcom. And so, the rest of the week went by, and Raven got used to living on her own.

There were times when it delighted her – cleaning up seemed so much simpler, and she could walk around her pyjamas, or underwear, or nothing at all. But there were also times when it was lonely. That was to be expected, of course. She found herself speaking her thoughts out loud, singing in the kitchen, and sometimes narrating what she was doing. Arden called her most days, but the tinny distortion of his voice was a far cry from the solid weight of his physical presence.

One week later, Raven stood in front of her full-length mirror, contemplating her outfit. She had on a short, grey dress with long sleeves, and dark stockings. Her faded leather boots that she wore day in, day out, she exchanged for a sleek pair of heels. Her deep, wine-coloured lipstick brought out the slight blue pallor of her pale skin. Finally, she slid her arms and wings through the soft folds of a custom-made, black velvet coat. And then she was ready.

Elias met her at The Rainbow Connection again, in jeans and rolled-up sleeves. Nerves fluttered in Raven's belly as he saw her and smiled – he really was very cute.

"Hello, beautiful lady," he said in greeting, kissing her cheek. Then, before he pulled away, he said in her ear, "You look incredible tonight."

They had a couple of drinks, and then a couple more as Elias pulled her from place to place, in a string of cosy, hipster bars. Some were loud and raucous, some were hidden away and made signature cocktails. He didn't let her pay for any of her drinks, made her laugh a little too loudly, and when he spoke about the PhD he was doing in renewable energy, it was difficult not to be impressed.

With Elias, the concrete somehow sprouted colour. He knew the city so well, knew where to find alleys full of neon lights, restaurants with candles and chequered tablecloths, and bricks dressed up in rainbow aerosol. Even the streetlights suddenly seemed not just white but blue or yellow, and Raven was quietly delighted at having a local to show her around. *This* was the way to get to know a city. As they went, Raven added and added to the map in her head. And she was charmed by Repanthe and Elias in equal measure.

Finally, they settled in a dimly-lit bar that used tall barrels as tables. The ground floor had people crammed in like sardines, but Elias had led her round the back and up a flight of narrow stairs. Upstairs, it was nearly empty. There were a handful of people scattered around, but it was quiet. Soft music floated among wisps of muted conversation. This level even had its own bartender, a muscly satyr in a black satin waistcoat and white shirtsleeves. He looked up as they reached the top of the stairs, and winked at Raven.

There was a bench top running along the far side of the room, and Elias picked up their drinks, and pulled her into one of the stools there.

"I've saved the best till last," Elias said. "The Rainbow Connection is my local, but for special occasions, this is my favourite place."

Raven looked around at the rich, mahogany furniture, the warm down-lights over the bar, the mounted moose head on the wall. It looked completely different from the cluttered downstairs.

"Is that real?" she asked, pointing to the moose.

"No idea," Elias replied. "We'll have to ask it later." He pushed her drink closer to her. "So, what do you think so far? Repanthe growing on you yet?"

"I think it is," Raven smiled. "This place is amazing. Although, I did also really like that third bar with the arcade games."

"Yeah, I like that one, too. Does your home town have this sort of thing?"

Raven snorted. "I think you know that it doesn't. Cressock has one pub, and it's mostly old men watching fae-league football."

"I like hearing you talk about that place," Elias said. "Sounds like a dream. I've lived in the city my whole life."

Raven sighed. "Well, I could go on and on."

"Please do." Elias picked up her hand and toyed with her fingers. "I'm woefully under-travelled." Her hands always seemed to be cold, but his were warm.

"What else do you want to know?"

"Mmm, tell me about the forest some more."

Raven rested her chin on her free hand, and her eyes stared off into the distance. It was so recently that she had left there, but it felt so far away.

"Well, it's pretty cold this time of year. Colder than here. But, in the forest, the trees are so thick it's actually pretty sheltered. There are some dangerous areas, but the fae beasts mostly hibernate, so winter is a great time to explore. And if you stay up all night, you can see the midnight flowers bloom."

Elias' fingers drifted up her bare forearm. Raven bit the inside of her cheek so she wouldn't shiver. He swivelled around on his stool and caged her knees with his.

"What are midnight flowers?" he asked. It was hard to concentrate while he was staring at her like this.

"They're lovely little things, they glow on the inside but you can only see them when they open up, and only when it's very dark. They open for an hour, at midnight, and the forest floor is just covered with them. A whole carpet of lights beneath your feet."

"Sounds beautiful," Elias murmured. He toyed with the end of her hair, near her elbow, and Raven watched his fingers.

"It is." She felt she might be babbling a bit. "And they're lighter than air, literally, so instead of dropping petals on the ground when they shed, they float up and away."

"I want to go on a hundred dates with you, just to hear your faerie stories."

Raven finally met his gaze again, and his gentle blue eyes tugged her closer. He leaned in, and pressed his lips to hers.

Elias tasted of lime, and gin, and very distantly of salt. It took a moment for Raven to realise she was holding her breath. She slid to the edge of her stool to kiss him again, and his hands pulled her in at the waist. They slid up between her wings and pressed into her back. She felt warm all over. She felt giddy. She felt a little in over her head.

Raven pulled back.

"Hey…" she said quietly. "I just want you to know that… I don't really go in for one-night-stands."

Elias reached between them, and pulled her stool in closer.

"Me neither," he said.

"I don't need a boyfriend," Raven clarified quickly. "I just… I mean it's never really worth it, right?" She bit her lip, feeling self-conscious for talking about sex.

But Elias just nodded seriously. "I'm not going anywhere," he murmured, and then kissed her again. "Let's take a walk."

He led Raven out of the bar and they strolled for a while, Elias again somehow finding quieter spaces even in the big city. At one point, he stopped on a corner and kissed her against the mossy side of a church, his mouth warm and the wall behind her cold through her coat.

"I live pretty close to here," Elias murmured. "Do you want to come check it out?"

Raven's pulse picked up.

She was definitely, absolutely sure this was a bad idea.

But the alcohol and his cologne chased each other in circles around her head, and it was so cold outside, and so empty in her house.

She nodded.

"Let's go."

Elias lived in a gorgeous apartment on the seventeenth floor. It was newer, shinier, and all around more expensive-looking than Raven's little set up. Elias threw his jacket over the counter, and then without further preamble tugged her into the bedroom. His bed was huge, and the heat of his skin on hers made her feel so much less alone. It was a feeling she could crawl into. He pressed her down on the cool sheets, laid his forearms on either side of her face, and kissed along her collarbone.

"Are you okay on your back?" he asked her. "You know, on your wings?"

Raven laughed. "Of course."

"Not something I usually have to think about myself," he said. He kissed her mouth, and smoothed one hand down her calf to hook her leg to his hip.

"You really are the most adorable little thing," he said. She put her hands over his jaw, feeling the rough stubble on his cheeks. The weight of another person's body pressing hers down felt like exhaling.

Soon, her dress and his shirt were on the floor, and the cold metal of his open zipper was biting into her bare stomach.

Sex with Elias was not mind-blowing, but it made her miss home a little less. Afterwards, he lay against her chest and breathed deeply, and Raven listened to the quick, strong beat of his human heart.

All in all, finding Elias had been easy. Raven smiled in the dark, and felt a thrill of pride at this proof that she could exist in the city, and be seen, and even liked. The feeling of new beginnings was a warm glow under her ribs, and she stroked his hair as he twitched in his sleep. The sex would be better the next time, anyway.

The following morning, Raven perched on the granite countertop while Elias fed her big, fat strawberries.

"Next date, I'll make you a real breakfast," he told her.

"I rather like fruit," Raven replied. Elias picked up a strawberry.

"The tip of the strawberry is the sweetest part," he said. "You have to eat it in two bites to taste the difference." He put the over-sized fruit to Raven's lips, then pulled her legs around his waist and kissed her before she swallowed so strawberry juice ran between them.

Raven spent the rest of the weekend in the library. She re-shelved books, a tedious but not difficult task. At one point she put away books about generating energy, and thought of Elias. It made her smile – as one of the Folk, the earth would always be important to her, and she liked that it seemed important to Elias, too. Whether they would just be casual or something more.

She learned to use the extensive university databases, and wandered the stacks in awe. Despite the bustling student population, there were enough books here that she could walk back and forth between the towering shelves, and barely see a soul. To her great delight, there was a whole section on fae literature, albeit not an especially large section. She would have to show this to Nola.

On Monday, everyone filed into class. Nola and Dev sat on either side of Raven, and whispered across to her while a representative from the student council gave a presentation about university clubs and societies.

"Soooo," Dev said. "How'd the date go?"

Without meaning to, Raven smiled. "It went really well. I wasn't even thinking about dating when I moved here, but I had a good time."

"Are you going to see him again?" Nola asked.

"I think so," said Raven. "We went to some great bars, maybe we could all go next time."

"That's great!" said Dev. "How was his dick?"

"Dev!"

"What? You had sex, right?"

Raven blushed.

"That's a yes," Dev confirmed. "If you're old enough to have sex, you're old enough to talk about dick."

"Dev, come on, she's clearly uncomfortable," Nola interrupted.

"Well, this is a safe place to learn to get comfortable with these things. It's very freeing, Raven. Come on, say it with me. *Diiiiiick.*"

Nola reached around Raven and smacked Dev upside the head.

"Ignore this asshole. Was he nice to you?"

Raven smiled. "Yeah, he was."

"That's all I was checking, too," Dev said, rubbing his head with a frown. "Sorry for saying 'dick' so many times."

Nola patted his hair absently, and Dev immediately reached up and pulled it back into place. "Did you set another date?"

"No, he said he didn't know what was happening with work this week, but that he'd text me when he did."

"Well, if you want, you can invite him to my gig this weekend," Dev said.

"You play in a band?" Nola asked.

"Yes! Well, sort of. Me and Josh have been talking about it for ages, and yesterday he met this girl at *Wild Things* who says she could sing lead. So, we're meeting up this week and then going to an open mic night on Saturday."

"Okay so... you've never played together," Raven hedged.

"No, but we can practice like, every day," Dev said.

"Dev, have either of you actually heard this girl sing?" Nola asked.

"No, but Josh says she has one of those really short fringes like the indie rock girls, so I think she'd be a good fit for us."

"Right," Raven said. "Well. I will certainly... tell Elias,

when I see him. But he might already have plans for us, last time he did all the organising."

But by the end of the week, Raven still hadn't heard from him. She tried not to think about it too much, but when she realised her favourite lipstick was missing, she sent off a quick text.

Hey Elias. Hope your week is going well. Did I leave my lipstick at your place, by any chance?

She upturned her bag over the bed and rifled through the contents, but to no avail. The weekend passed, he never replied.

Everything okay?

Still, nothing. Raven played his words over in her head. *I want to go on a hundred dates with you, just to hear your faerie stories. Next date, I'll make you a real breakfast.*

I'm not going anywhere.

"Maybe he's really busy?" she said to Nola and Dev. They looked sceptically at her.

"Sounds like he's ghosting you, hun," Nola said.

"Men are the worst," Dev said, shaking his head. "What a curse it is, to be born loving men."

"*Dating* is the worst," Nola corrected. "Girls are slightly nicer, but honestly not that much. I've been ghosted by both. But, yes, men are also the worst," she added.

"But why would he do that?" Raven frowned. "We had a really good time. We had breakfast, he said he wanted to see me again."

"So, he lied," Dev supplied.

"He lied," Raven repeated, her face contorting with disgust. "But there was no point, I was already going home with him. That's not *clever*, that's… that's…"

"It's terribly uncouth and not at all creative," Nola sniffed.

"But that's what Repanthe men are like. They will be sweet as sugar for as long as it takes to get what they want, they'll lie because that's what humans do, and then they disappear. Worst part is, they make you breakfast on the way out so they don't have to feel guilty about it, and then you feel like somehow it's your fault."

"Yeah, you know why I'm still with my dumbass boyfriend?" Dev said. "He's the only one who actually wanted a relationship, and I'm not trawling through a string of one-night stands to find that again."

"But I didn't ask for a relationship," Raven said. "I just want... not to be treated like I'm disposable."

Nola nodded. "I know, sweet pea. Welcome to the big city."

Raven put her head down on the desk. It had been a month since she had arrived in the city, and apparently this was what it looked like to really get to know Repanthe.

Two

The Incident

OVER THE next few weeks, Raven got to know the important landmarks of the city: less-frequented routes to the university, tailors that altered human clothing for the Folk, and cheap restaurants that did home delivery. She even went on a couple of dates, but Elias had left a bad taste in her mouth. Raven, like all faerie children, was well-practiced in picking apart half-truths and deceptions. But when Elias had lied, there was nothing clever for her to unravel — just the crude fabrication. And if they all seemed nice at first, if they all could point-blank lie, how could you trust any of them?

No matter, Raven was supposed to be making her way on her own, anyway. She tried to force herself not to be bothered by it.

Raven called home every weekend to check in with her parents and younger siblings. She was the eldest of four, but the next oldest faeling was eight when she moved out of home, so she loved them dearly but wasn't necessarily close to them.

On Tuesdays, Arden video-called her.

"Hey, Lightfoot!" he said cheerily.

"Hey, Sliver."

"You all right?"

"I'm all right."

"How are the humans treating you?"

She wriggled in the armchair, banishing the thought of Elias.

"I've only met a few. I did meet Dev's boyfriend last weekend. Josh."

"Josh? That's such a human name."

Raven laughed. Dating was hard, but this was easy. "I know. How's everyone back home?"

"Eh, same old same old," Arden said. "Asher's fang teeth are coming in, so he's a right little shit at the moment."

Raven smiled at the memory of Arden's teenage brother. "Ah, puberty," she said.

"Indeed," Arden said, dryly. "He's been hanging out here because at home he keeps fighting with Mum. But I don't want him here either, he's eating me out of house and home."

"Yeah, that runs in the family," Raven smirked.

"Yeah, well, I pay for my own food and wouldn't mind if he just went through that. But he's eating *everyone's* food. The other housemates are starting to turn on me."

"Ooh, have you filled my room yet?"

"Luckily, we have. Asher's been trying to convince me to let him move in. There's no way his fifteen-year-old ass is living with me."

"Do tell," Raven prompted.

"Remember Jade, the gremlin with the mohawk?"

"Oh yeah, she had that human girlfriend in high school, right?"

"Apparently she's not heaps keen on that being the thing she's known for, but yeah, her. She's moving in. Next week, I think. And speaking of replacing friends, are you going to virtually introduce me to Nola and Dev yet?"

Raven made a face. "They're not replacement friends, don't even joke."

"Either way, I want to see your fancy city friends."

"All right, well, they're coming for dinner on Saturday. I can put you in the kitchen while we make food?"

"Deal."

And so, four days later, Raven had her phone perched on a cabinet, while the three friends squeezed around each other trying to make dinner in the tiny house. After a while, Dev gave up and took his mixing bowl to sit on the staircase. Nola shut the oven and went to sit by the fire. Raven stayed and washed a few things in the sink.

"Hey!" came Arden's mechanical-sounding voice. "I can't see any of you."

Raven picked up with phone with her elbows, trying not to get it wet with her soapy hands, and plonked it in Nola's lap.

"Here, talk to Nola."

"Hey, girl!" Arden said. "What are you doing in the human city?"

"Same as everyone else," Nola replied. "Trying to get a slice of the pie, changing the system from the inside. This sort of thing."

"How do you stand the smell?" Arden asked. "I was there a week and had to wash all my clothes twice."

Back in the kitchen, Dev came and sat on the bench top. He handed Raven the mixing bowl.

"Hey, are you okay after the Elias stuff?" Dev asked.

Raven looked up in surprise. "Yeah," she said. "I barely knew the guy, don't worry about it."

Dev cocked his head. "I know I joke about sex, but I get the hurt, too. I think you can have very high highs and very low lows, in love and lust. And you didn't deserve what you got."

Raven stopped moving for a minute.

"It doesn't feel great," she admitted. Dev nodded. Somehow,

with Nola out of earshot it was easier to say out loud. "I feel like such an idiot. He played me and it was just *so* easy, you know?" Dev nodded again.

"You're not an idiot for believing him. You had no reason not to."

"I know that... cognitively. But my ego is bruised. And I'm still kinda mad."

"I get it," Dev said. "You *should* be mad." Raven sighed.

"Well, anyway. I don't think I want to date any more, at least for a bit." Dev nodded again, and Raven gave him a small smile in thanks. She resumed cooking.

After a moment, Dev said, "Raven, can I ask you some stuff about the Folk?"

"Sure," said Raven, adding the mix to the pan.

"I don't want to be offensive; I just don't have a lot of fae friends and I figure better to find out than to assume and fuck it up."

"That makes sense. Shoot."

"Okay. What's the iron thing? Are fae killed by iron?"

Raven laughed, then looked up and realised Dev was being serious.

"Oh, ah, no it doesn't kill us. It smells pretty bad, and might give you a rash if you rub it on your skin. Kind of like..." She searched for a suitable analogy. "Ammonia? You can use it every day, but you're not about to take a bath in it."

Dev nodded. "Right, makes sense. The lying thing?"

"Physically impossible. Fae can't lie."

"Wow. And you aren't... immortal?"

Raven stared at him.

"Do humans really think this stuff?"

Dev looked sheepish. "No, but there are rumours. I've just

45

never really gotten to ask someone before."

Raven sighed. "Okay, well, I think we might have a slightly longer life span, depending on the race. But definitely not immortal. What else have you got?"

"Do you have a fae name as well as your normal name?"

"Yes, all fae have a true name and a given name."

"What's your true name?"

"Oh. I can't tell you that. You actually can't ask that; it's considered pretty rude."

"I'm sorry," Dev said.

"That's fine, you didn't know. Just don't ask anyone else unless you want your ass kicked. Anything else?"

"One more. This is going to sound really dumb, but… can you do magic?"

"There used to be a lot of magic," Raven told him. "But after the Realm War, magic was outlawed until it was all but forgotten. I think there's a little in some remote communities, but, mostly, no. I certainly don't know any." She tilted her head to one side. "Don't they teach you this stuff in high school?"

Dev shook his head. "Not in the city. I mean we learn about the Realm War and human colonisation, but we sort of skim over the details."

"Well, that's not great. There's a fae literature section in the library, I'll show you next time we're in there. It was pretty brutal, they dismantled the Seelie Court and pretty much killed anyone who was loyal to the Queen. Then of course she was publicly beheaded anyway. They outlawed magics and fae languages…"

"Do you speak any fae?"

"Only a little," Raven said. "There used to be like two hundred different fae languages. Some words have stuck around.

Like, for example, we mostly use the Gregorian calendar from the human realm, right? Well, we actually had our own calendar. And six seasons, which is why the four seasons don't always fit the weather patterns."

"Like how the first month of summer it's just incredibly rainy," Dev supplied.

"Exactly. So back home, we mostly speak like you do, but sometimes with fae words. Like, the days of the week. Nola does this too."

Dev looked mystified.

"I hadn't even noticed. What are the days of the week in fae?"

Raven counted on her fingers.

"Ishtak, Nyetak, Only, Swiftak, Grimstak, Inktak, Oftak. Luckily, we have seven, too."

"That's so cool, I didn't know."

"There's a good story behind it, too. They say that back in the war, fae prisoners were punished for speaking their own languages. Then, some prisoners planned a daring escape, and the guards found out. They got one of them in an interrogation room and tried to torture him for information. They already had most of the plan, just not when it was going to happen. The prisoner gave the days in fae, and bought the rest of them enough time to escape. So now the day names are still in our slang."

Dev looked both impressed and slightly horrified.

"Is that true?" he asked.

Raven shrugged. "There are lots of stories. I can give you some books, if you're interested."

"Okay that'd be great, thanks. Hey, sorry if those are awkward questions."

"That's all right. You're right, better that you ask than make

47

assumptions."

"Do you want to ask me anything about humans?"

Raven thought for a second. "I don't think so? I mean, we grew up with human media and stuff so it doesn't seem so foreign."

"Oh. Right."

"But I'll let you know if I think of anything," Raven added quickly, seeing Dev's face fall. "Hey, can you mash these potatoes?"

Dev puffed his chest out. "Potatoes, root vegetables from the human realm. Once the scourge of a carb-fearing world, potatoes have revived in popularity since being imported into the fae realm. They are cheap, easy to grow, and all-round delicious."

Raven raised an eyebrow, and said nothing.

"Just trying to teach you something in return."

Raven blinked.

"Yes, mash, can do, I am the Queen of mash." Dev grabbed up the masher and got to work.

In the small sitting room, Raven had put a low coffee table in the centre in lieu of a full-sized dining table. They sat on the floor around it to eat.

"Okay, Arden, time for dinner. Say goodbye."

"Goodbye, Raven's hot friend!" Dev chirped, waving the masher and splattering bits of potato across the table. Raven turned the phone around so that everyone could see Arden waving, then hung up.

One Saturday night, Dev turned up at Raven's house in a tuxedo, with his bowtie undone and hanging open around his neck. She stood in the doorway with her toes curled under, while the wind gusted around them, whimpering and scratching to be let in.

"Raven, my lady, I bring you tidings of good cheer and expensive booze," he said, holding two large bottles aloft.

"Dev, what are you doing here? Are you drunk right now?" she asked.

"Verily, I say unto thee, I am not," he replied. "Although I don't remember how I got here, or where Josh is, or where my coat might be. I'm coming in."

He stumbled inside uninvited, and Raven frowned. She had forgotten that threshold protections, like her ivy and rowan wreath, did not work on humans.

Raven followed him in. "It's freezing out. Where have you come from?"

Dev sashayed across the room, placing the bottles heavily on the kitchen counter and stumbling into the armchair.

"My parents are hosting a gala dinner at the house. I got bored, and I guess I wandered off. But they live pretty far away, so that doesn't explain how I got here exactly..." His eyes widened. "You have wings! Did we fly here?"

Before she could think of an answer to the nonsensical question, Raven's phone rang.

"Raven, Josh is calling me. Is Dev there?"

"Yeah, he's here."

"Who's that?" Dev mouthed. "Is it Josh?"

"No," she told him, "it's Nola. Josh is calling her."

"Great," Nola said, grumpily. "Can you tell him to stop giving out my number? I did not consent to this."

"Nola says to stop giving out her number."

"You know, I don't remember giving anyone her number."

"Well, you also don't remember crossing the city to get here, so excuse me if I don't take your word for it."

"Wait," said Nola, suddenly interested. "Is he wasted?"

"Oh, yeah. He just turned up here, no coat or anything. Just two bottles of scotch."

"Ooh I bet it's the good stuff too. His parents are loaded. I'll be right there."

Twenty minutes later, Raven and Nola stood in the kitchen watching Dev run in tight circles around the tiny living room, flapping his arms and trying to fly home.

"Humans have a truly tiny alcohol tolerance," Nola said.

"What are we supposed to do with this?" Raven asked.

"There's only one thing to do," Nola responded. She picked up a bottle of scotch, and handed the other to Raven. "Join in."

By the time the first bottle was empty and they were half way through the second, Dev had tired himself out. The three of them were lying on the shag pile rug in front of the fire, with their heads in the middle and their feet making a rough sort of circle on the outside.

"This is the circle of truth," Dev said, slurring his words. "We should all tell each other a secret."

"What kind of secret?" Raven asked.

"I don't know. A secret you haven't told anyone before."

"You go first, Dev," Nola said. "Give us an example."

"Okay," said Dev. A hiccup escaped him. "My secret it, I didn't leave the party because I was bored. I left because I saw Josh kissing someone else."

Raven sat up. "Aw Dev, that's terrible," she said.

"No, it's okay, we actually agreed that it's okay to kiss other people."

Raven lay back down. "Then why did you leave?"

"Because, I lied. I don't want him kissing other people. It feels terrible. I'm jealous and sad all the time."

"Again with the humans and the lying," Raven muttered.

"So why don't you tell him?" Nola asked.

"Because I'm trying to be this cool, open-minded person," Dev said. "Dating is hard."

"I don't think you have to be any kind of person you don't want to be. But dating *is* hard," Nola agreed. She took a deep breath. "My secret is, I'm seeing a human who lives downtown."

"Why is that a secret?" Dev asked.

Nola shrugged. "I kind of thought I'd end up with someone fae, because it'd be easier. But this human has the most beautiful soul. Problem is, his parents don't approve of him dating a non-human. He hasn't told them about me."

"What?" said Raven. "You're adults, why do his parents get any say in who he dates?"

Nola took a drink. "I said the same thing. But it turns out, his brother ran away with a fae boy. And they cut him out. Like of the family, of the will, everything. Kofi's still close to him, and he's been trying to repair the relationship for years. But they won't budge. They have a grandchild they've never even met. He says he's just waiting for the right time, but I can tell he's actually really afraid of losing them, too."

Raven was appalled. "Nola, I'm so sorry."

"What can I do? Obviously I don't want to be a secret, but I don't want him to lose his family, either."

They were all quiet for a moment.

"What about you, Raven?" Dev said. "Dating embargo still in place?"

"Yep," was all Raven said.

"No one tempting?" he asked.

"Nope," Raven replied.

"What about Arden?"

"What *about* Arden?"

51

"He's a straight-up babe," Dev said. "Why aren't you with him?"

"He's my best friend," Raven responded automatically. "We've known each other since birth."

"So?" Dev took a mouthful of scotch.

"I'm actually with Dev on this one," Nola said. "Best friends make wonderful lovers. But, also, I don't buy into the whole 'men and women can't be friends' shit. Are you not into him like that?"

"Don't be ridiculous," Raven said, a little too defensively. She flushed. Both her friends looked at her.

Raven sighed. "It's hard for me to talk about. This isn't something I've spoken about to anyone, especially not Arden."

Dev handed her the bottle. *"Circle of truuuuth,"* he crooned.

Raven drank. "I'm not sure where to begin." She passed the bottle back to Dev, and watched the room spin slowly above her. "Arden is my very best friend. We were born on the same day, and so I can truly say I have loved him my whole life. But just as my best friend. And then... a couple of months ago..."

"What?" Dev breathed.

"A couple of months ago, we had... The Incident. And it really scared me."

"What was the incident?" Nola asked.

"I guess... we had... a moment."

"Like, a *sexy* moment?" Dev squealed.

Raven squirmed uncomfortably. "It's not that simple. I realised that I have no idea how to love Arden like that. And more to the point, I don't know if I want to."

"Is who we love a choice we make?" Nola said.

"It's a choice who we're with," Raven said firmly. "I don't want to be that small town girl who marries the boy next door and gets stuck there forever. Arden looks after his mum, and his little brother, and has never thought about leaving." She took deep breath. "Besides, we were pretty drunk at the time. Maybe we didn't mean it. The next day, we both acted like nothing happened. Actually, I'm not even sure Arden remembers it, he was so hung over."

"You never talked about it?" Dev asked.

"How you do bring something like that up?" Raven returned. "It would have changed everything. It was good the way it was. Then before I could really make a decision, I got my acceptance from the university. It seemed like a sign. I packed my bags and came out here a week later."

"I don't put much stock into signs," Nola mused. "But if it's what you wanted, then I'm glad you came."

"I'm not sure what I want," Raven admitted. "But I think that's the point. I'm twenty-one and I've lived in Cressock my entire life. I want to become my own whole person, before I wind up hitched to the literal first man I ever met."

"But…" Dev stuttered. "What if he's your soulmate?"

"No," Nola said. "I get it. Be your own person, and not just half of someone else."

"Exactly," Raven said. "I'm happy to be here. It's where I need to be."

Dev looked around the room, his eyes settling on the framed picture of a snow-dusted Raven and Arden. Arden was smiling at the camera, his chin on the top of her head, and Raven had her eyes creased shut in laughter. They looked happier than he and Josh had ever been.

"You must miss him," he said.

"You have no idea."

"Hey. Yuletide break is only six weeks away," Nola said.

"Yeah," Raven closed her eyes. "I can't wait."

Finally telling people about this gave Raven a sense of relief, at first. Everyone back home knew the both of them so well, she didn't feel like she could talk to anyone about it. And when Arden had acted completely normally towards her the next day, she had followed suit. It was like it had never happened. But now, speaking the words out loud, The Incident came screaming back to the forefront of her memory. And suddenly the mortifying images were all there in front of her. She grabbed the scotch back and drained the bottle.

The next morning, Raven woke up to the sound of her phone vibrating underneath her. They had fallen asleep on the rug, and the fire had died.

"Hello?" Her voice sounded scratchy in her own ears, and she scrabbled around for a throw to wrap around herself.

"Lightfoot! You sound like shit, did I wake you?"

"Hey, Arden. What time is it?"

"It's eleven, sleeping beauty. Up and at 'em. I've got good news."

Raven dragged herself upright and started looking for spare blankets for Nola and Dev, still sleeping soundly on the floor.

"Oh yeah, what's that?"

"I'm coming to visit you!"

Raven stopped walking. "You are?"

"Yeah, I'm in the car right now!"

"Wait, you're coming today?"

"Sure am. Finally finished that fancy-ass cabinet for my client in Linkhaven and he's paying extra for delivery. So, I'll be passing through Repanthe in about an hour."

"That's amazing!" Raven yelled. She glanced quickly back

at her friends, but they didn't stir.

"I know! I was trying to keep it a surprise but I got too excited."

Raven laughed, more quietly this time. "I'm excited too. How long will you have?"

"Probably won't stay too long, I want to get to Linkhaven before the sun goes down."

"Well that sucks. Guess I'll take whatever time I can get. See you in a few."

"Bye, kid."

Raven hugged her arms around herself. In just sixty little minutes, Arden would be here and the world would be right again.

Suddenly, the conversation from the night slammed back into Raven's mind, and her face fell. For the first time since it actually happened, The Incident had been let out of its cage, and flashbulb snapshots of that night shoved themselves in front of her eyes: Arden's fingers against the skin of her back. Her barely-there silver dress. The way his eyes had looked in the dark.

Raven shook her head, and gripped the throw around her shoulders tighter to her. She just had to keep moving. She brought the heater from her bedroom down for Dev and Nola, so they could wake up warm. She traipsed up the stairs and plugged her phone in, then took a very hot shower. She washed the smell of scotch and fire from her hair, and scrubbed yesterday's makeup from her eyes. She whirled around her bedroom, putting underwear back into drawers and stacking books into orderly piles on her dresser.

By the time Raven got back downstairs, in a fresh set of soft black tights and oversized sweater, Dev and Nola were moving slowly around the room.

"Morning," Nola said, folding blankets.

"Morning, you two," Raven said. "How is everyone?"

"Confused," said Dev, yawning hugely. "How did I get here?"

Raven smirked. "I honestly have no idea. You live across town and turned up at my doorstep without so much as a coat."

Dev stopped in his tracks. "I did?" He patted his pockets. "I don't even have my phone. How much did I drink last night?"

"Come on," Nola said, coming up behind him. "My car's here, I'll take you home." She turned to Raven. "What are you up to today?"

"Well," said Raven, wiping her hands on her pants. "Arden is actually coming over, in…" she looked over at the clock on the oven, and panic rose in her throat. "Fifteen minutes."

Dev's eyes bulged. "Was I hammered last night or do I remember you telling us you had a thing with him and then almost immediately moved here and have barely seen him since?"

Nola rolled her eyes. "Both. Now march." She took his shoulders and steered him towards the door, looking back to mouth 'good luck' to Raven on their way out. Raven shot her a grateful look, and closed the door on the sound of Dev hollering, "Thanks for looking after me," as Nola towed him away.

The silence rang in her ears. Fifteen minutes stretched out before her like a desert, and Raven paced up and down the tiny house nervously. Memories of The Incident had their claws in her brain, and she had to get this under control before Arden got in. *Come on, pull it together,* she told herself. They had survived their joint birthday and the friendship had carried on like normal for two weeks. Then they had had their longest separation of their lives. Raven was hoping that that would put The Incident farther behind them, but now it was rearing its horrifying head once again. *Why* had she told her friends about this? Why had she said the words out loud?

The knock at the door made Raven jump as if it were a gunshot. She stood still, and forced herself to take three deep breaths. *It's just Arden,* she told herself. *Remember Arden? That little boy who made sandcastles with you. That dumb teenager who fell out of a tree and broke his arm. That man who is still your best friend.* Raven exhaled slowly, and opened the door.

Arden stood there, with his lovely, familiar features stretched into a big, goofy grin, and a huge bunch of yellow flowers in his hands. Raven's heart stopped.

"Surprise!" he yelled.

"It's not a surprise, you massive dork, you called me and told me you were coming." She touched the door wreath and invited him in, putting her nose into the bouquet. They matched the colour of his eyes.

"Those are from my mum. She says hi."

"Thanks, Annabelle," Raven said, putting them in a vase while Arden walked past her. "That's so lovely of her, to be thinking about me while your crazy brother's running—"

Raven had set the flowers down and was turning to head into the sitting room, but as soon as she was facing him, Arden stepped forward and folded her into his enormous arms. She stopped mid-sentence, and stood still. For a second, the warmth of him, the feel of his soft, grey hair on her cheek, the absolutely perfect scent of him, overwhelmed her. She loved him so much it physically hurt her chest. Then, as her arms came up over the mountains of his shoulders, she relaxed. How could she feel discomfort in Arden's embrace? This was home to her. So, she breathed him in deeply, leaned against his solid bulk, and closed her eyes against the flannel of his shirt.

The rest of the afternoon went by relatively smoothly. They ate grilled cheese sandwiches, and drank hot, bitter tea that Raven's dad had sent with Arden. Raven went out to the truck to see Arden's finished cabinet. It was a thing of beauty, and Raven fawned over it until Arden blushed.

"It's come up all right," he said gruffly.

"It's amazing," Raven said. "You've been doing this, what, six months now?"

"Yeah, turns out I quite like cabinet making."

"I'm glad. You were wasted on building houses."

"I like houses too. I like the idea that the thing I'm making is going to be lived in. But this was a really good project."

Raven ran her hand over the ivy carved in relief over the doors. "I would live in here if I could."

"Well, thanks. Hopefully Mr Montague likes it, too."

"Lachlan must be pleased."

Arden made a face. "You know my uncle, he's never pleased."

"He's grumpy, but he thinks you're good. Have you taken him up on that manager role yet?"

Arden locked up the ute and they strolled back to the house.

"Nah. I don't want the extra responsibility. Just want to turn up, build shit, then go home again. I've seen how long he stays back, and it does not seem appealing."

They went back inside, and Arden draped his long frame over the armchair.

"So," he said, "you're two months in now. What do you think of life in the big smoke?"

Raven smiled. "There's lots to love. Nola and Dev are great, I'm so attached to my little house. Living on my own makes me feel like I'm finally a real adult." She paused.

"But?" Arden prompted.

"But I don't think I realised how different it was going to be from home. I like how crazy busy it is. But it's *always* that busy. Like you can't just take an easy walk down the street, there's a crowd to contend with, every single day. So many people, but if none of them know who you are, you're still alone. And that's somehow more lonely than being lonely on your own. It's kind of exhausting." She didn't mention Elias.

"And I knew it was going to be human central," Raven continued, "but there are *so. Many. Humans.* Like where are all the Folk? I've got Nola, but she's pretty much the only fae I know. Getting to know Dev has been fascinating. He walked straight in here the other day, no invitation no nothing."

"Well, that's sort of horrifying. Don't get robbed."

Raven ignored the last comment. "Did you know that they don't learn about fae oppression in history class here?"

Arden snorted. "No, but it really doesn't surprise me."

"How can they not teach that stuff?"

"I don't know, but it makes sense that in city with the highest human population, they wouldn't rag on about what terrible people their ancestors were."

"I guess. But that kind of makes it worse. At least they sort of acknowledge it at uni. I'm thinking about doing my final presentation on impacts of colonisation on health in fae communities."

"Great idea. At least that one class will have some idea of what really happened."

The minutes ticked by and then all too soon, Arden had to leave. Raven clung to him in the doorway, and buried her face in his chest. He hugged her tightly, dropped a kiss on her head, and then he was gone.

That week, missing Arden was a gaping hole in her chest, shocking her with the pain of it. Raven pushed hard against the memories of The Incident. She concentrated on her uni work, and turned in a polished five-thousand-word essay. She worked extra hours in the library, paid her rent and then tucked what was left over into an envelope at the back of her bedside drawer. She made a note to open a city bank account, after Arden's comment about getting robbed. She went dancing with Nola and some of her friends in a hidden fae club that was unmarked on the outside but raucous on the inside. And eventually, she managed to get The Incident back into the box in her mind where it was kept. By Friday, she was drained, but her emotions were under control. Luckily, Arden had to skip that week's video call due to a work commitment, and the space from him was a relief.

Over the weekend, Raven walked with Nola around the more fae parts of the city. Although everything was still concrete and iron, Raven noticed that in in certain quarters the plants had begun to fight back, and shoots of greenery poked irrepressibly through cracks in the pavement and in old walls. There were even wildflowers growing in some corners, and Raven was quietly proud of them.

In the big open spaces, there were always flocks of tourists, but they had trouble navigating some of the more transient pathways. One particular human, an older woman, stopped them and asked for help.

"Excuse me," she said very loudly. Her mouth moved with exaggerated enunciation. "Do either of you speak the human tongue?"

"Yes," said Nola through gritted teeth. Raven grimaced and

wondered how it was that this person thought their language would be vastly different, but not that larger fae ears might mean more sensitive hearing. Despite Nola's affirmation, the woman continued to shout.

"We are looking for Asteria Road." She flapped a map in front of their faces, and the human man with her chimed in. Also loudly.

"We are LOST," he said. "Can you HELP US?"

"On one condition," Nola said. "That you lower your gods-damned voices." The woman looked slightly shocked, but managed to hand the map over without saying anything. "Asteria street is just on the end of the block. It's a shy street," Nola explained. "See how it's a dotted line on the map? That means it's shy."

"What do you mean, shy?" the man asked.

"You know. Easily startled," Raven supplied. "Just approach it slowly." The humans just stared. Nola sighed.

"Okay. In the Fae Realm, some streets are a little shy. You can't see them unless you come up slowly, and it helps to keep your eyes down. I should also tell you that dashed lines on the map, like this one," Nola traced her finger down the map, "are sly streets. Sly streets are like the opposite of shy streets, they start out clear but if they know you're coming they disappear. With sly streets it's best to surprise them. Pretend to be walking one direction then make a sudden turn before it catches you."

The human man blinked. "Young lady, are you making fun of us?"

"No," Nola said patiently. "Here, look."

She walked up the block and slowed down near a steampunk-themed cafe. She kept her gaze downcast, and then turned and disappeared through a crack in the wall. The human couple screamed.

Nola reappeared, and joined them. "See?" she said. "It'll make more sense when you get up close, you can see the street from front on. Go on."

The tourists looked at each other and then held hands tightly, tiptoeing like cartoon characters up to the same crack in the wall with pale faces.

"No, you don't have to—" Raven began, but Nola shushed her.

"They'll figure it out," she said. "Come on, let's keep going."

"They don't have transient roads in the human realm?" Raven asked.

"They do not."

After that encounter, Raven decided to get out of the city to stretch her wings and clear her mind. She spent Saturday evening researching the area, then on Sunday morning caught a train out to the foothills to the north of Repanthe. There was a small town here, where Raven bought a couple of snacks that she stuffed in her pockets for later. The sun was out, unusual for this time of year, but very welcome.

Raven followed a hiking trail away from the village. The path was overgrown with weeds, and loose stones threatened to turn her ankle. Lucky she wasn't planning on doing too much walking. A short way in, Raven's phone died, but she had an excellent sense of direction so it didn't worry her too much. At the top of a hill, she took a deep breath, and turned her face up to the weak, cusp-of-winter sun. The cold air thrilled her lungs, and a breeze rustled her hair. That was what she was waiting for.

Sure enough, the wind picked up a moment later, and she

leapt and snapped her wings open. Raven had timed it well, so she only had to beat her wings a couple of times to get her into the air. The wind did the rest. She coasted along with a playful easterly, and was buffeted up higher, and higher. Her wings were slightly stiff; this was the first decent flight she'd had since moving to the city. But it was wonderful to be out in the open, away from the stench of iron and the hampering telephone cables. The sunlight through her iridescent wings scattered rainbows on the grass beneath her. The city fell far away, and the sky threw open its arms to her.

Raven soared over a small forest, and tiny sparrows rose to meet her. She chirruped at them, and they darted around her excitedly. She flew low over a rushing river and followed its winding length for a while. The icy spray tickled her wings, and she dodged the giant carp that jumped and snapped at her like some kind of overlarge insect. Her lungs felt strong in her chest, and even when a cold front sliced at her cheekbones, she felt giddy with joy. Raven closed her eyes, and tumbled around a few times. There was nothing in her mind but the sun on her skin, and the clean, sharp air in her chest.

At this altitude, life on the ground seemed to matter very little. Raven had always gone flying when she had felt stressed; it was a strategy her father had encouraged when she was little and her temper was taller than she was. Back in Cressock, she had occasionally gone flying with friends. On one memorable occasion, she and Jasper Jones had snuck out of geography class and flown high above the school grounds to make out. It had seemed like such a good idea at the time, but kissing and hovering had proved exceptionally difficult and they had almost fallen clean out of the sky.

Mostly, though, Raven liked to fly alone. The meditation of

the changing winds in her hair and beneath her wings was always enough to drive out the dull roar of her thoughts, and she used to be able to fly for hours at a time. Now, she closed her eyes and put her arms out wide, happy to be buffeted any way the wind wanted to take her.

Until she flew right into a low-hanging cloud.

Raven's eyes snapped open as she became instantly drenched. Sodden, her wings were suddenly three times as heavy, and she worked to make a slow and even decent. She shook herself off once on the ground, and looked around. She was not far from the train station, but she'd have to walk – there was no way she had the fitness to fly that distance with soaked wings. Then she'd have to sit on a train dripping wet, and shiver her way back to the city. Raven grinned. *Totally worth it.*

By the time Raven reached home, her teeth were chattering so hard she worried she could chip something. She stood in the shower until the hot water ran out, then towelled off and went to dry her wings in front of the heater. She plugged her phone in to charge, and started leafing through some readings for uni. She was just getting into a very interesting passage about early trials for PTSD treatments on survivors of the Realm War, when her phone buzzed to life. It buzzed so many times it nearly vibrated itself off the bedside table. Raven frowned. She didn't have that many friends; how could she have missed so many notifications in a few hours? She scrolled through the messages. Two missed calls from Dad, three from Mum. Six missed calls and thirteen texts from Arden. Raven's heart sped up. She wrapped her blanket around her shoulders and impatiently listened as his phone rang and rang. Finally, he picked up.

"Raven?" He sounded scared. Arden was almost never scared.

"Arden, what's going on?"

"Raven, you're okay. Fuck, I've been trying to get a hold of you all day."

"Why, what's happened? Is everyone all right?"

"Everyone here is fine. We just heard on the news about a shooting at a café. Not too far from the university. Three fae dead, one was a faerie. There was no other description but, fuck, Raven, how many faeries live in Repanthe city, right near the uni? Scared me half to death." His voice broke on the last word.

"Arden, oh, I'm so sorry. I'm absolutely fine. I didn't even know about the shooting, that's awful." She suddenly thought of Nola, and flicked open her social media page. Nola had recently shared a video of the breaking news. She was safe, too.

"Raven, I don't like you being there. Too many humans, too many guns. Why do people even have guns? I hadn't even thought about that." He groaned. "When are you coming home?"

"So soon," she said. "One more month."

"I don't know if I can wait that long," Arden said roughly.

"You already have," Raven soothed. "That's less than half the time I've been away. Just a few weeks more."

"I don't like this at all. I don't like being far away from you, I don't like not knowing if you're safe. I don't like not being able to hold you with my own two hands."

A memory, pulled from The Incident, flashed against the backs of here eyelids. Arden's hands, on both sides of her face. She pushed it down.

"I don't like it either," she admitted.

"So come home," Arden said tightly.

"Not yet, Arden. Soon."

Arden made a sound somewhere between a growl and a moan, long and low.

"You'd better make it home in one piece," he said. A wave of guilt crashed over her, for making him worry, for putting him through this. She had to remember very hard that untangling their lives was part of the reason she had left.

"I will."

A heavy silence settled between them.

"I'd better call Mum and Dad, too," Raven said eventually. "Tell them I'm okay."

"Yeah," said Arden. Neither of them moved.

"Raven?"

"Yeah?"

"I miss you."

Raven blinked furiously and willed herself not to cry. More memories spung up, unbidden. How warm it was in the crush of Arden's arms. The feel of his soft, wolfy ears between her fingers. His huge bulk and forest scent filling the cabin of his battered pick-up truck.

"I miss you, too," she said. The words scraped her throat on the way out.

That night, as she lay in bed, Raven wondered for the first time about her safety. Her being fae had caused difficulties for her, but it had never threatened her life before. She rolled over onto her back, and tried to think of something else. Which only led back to Arden. And before she could stop it, The Incident was spooling out in front of her.

The ache of missing Arden, that she had kept under wraps so well for the last couple of months, was made all too real by the knowledge that he was missing her, too. And so, in this weakened state, she was powerless to stop the flood of memories, and surrendered to watching them play out on the ceiling of the dark little room.

It was their twenty-first birthday party and the night was clear and full of stars. The house by the lake thrummed with life and laughter, buoyed by human champagne and faerie absinthe. Raven, in a scandalous silver dress that dipped low at the front and was cut away at the back, and with moonstones strewn through her masses of blue-black hair, threw back her head and laughed. The party was everything she wanted it to be.

Everyone from their high school was there, and Raven was dancing with a group of elves on the ground. Above them, roisterous pixies zoomed back and forth. She was pretty sure a couple of faeries were hooking up in the gargantuan bowl of the chandelier. Arden's brother Asher had tried to sneak in, but their mum had shown up and dragged him out by the scruff of the neck. Raven didn't care. Nothing could ruin this night.

Someone pushed through the crowded dance floor and yelled over the music that they were running low on drinks. Raven didn't remember who it was any more, but she did remember weaving through the crowd to the cellar. Let nobody say that she wasn't a good host. She remembered how abruptly the music cut out once the cellar door banged shut behind her. She remembered jumping when Arden bumped into her.

"What are you doing down here?" Raven asked in surprise. She had been facing the shelf of bottles, and when she spun around to face him, she tottered a little on her impractical shoes. She opened her wings slightly, for balance. Arden laughed.

"Are you drunk, Lightfoot?"

Raven stuck her tongue out at him. "I might be. Aren't you?"

"Oh, I definitely am. Faerie absinthe? I never stood a chance. Actually, I came to get more, they're all out upstairs."

"Me too," said Raven. "Looks like this is the last bottle."

She turned and reached for it, just as Arden took an unsteady step forward and did the same. The result was that Raven got squashed between the shelf and Arden – the wolfkin's whole body pressed up against hers, from where their hands touched over the green glass, and her wings dug into his chest, to his belt buckle against her lower back, and his jeans on the backs of her legs. Abruptly, the front of Raven's body felt cold, her flimsy dress only coming mid-thigh and providing no warmth in the underground cellar. Contrastingly, Arden's body was suddenly searing behind her.

They laughed awkwardly and Arden put his hand on Raven's waist to move her to the side, at the same time as Raven turned to let him through. The movement spun her torso against his outstretched fingers, and now they were face to face.

"Um," Arden swallowed, but found he couldn't shift his feet. They seemed to be encased in cement. Raven was breathing fast; he wasn't sure why she was but he was having a very hard time shifting his gaze from the too-quick up and down movements of her chest. Gods this dress was low.

Raven put a hand on Arden's chest. She meant to push him back, tried to laugh it off again, but there wasn't enough air down here. Instead, her fingers curled in his lapel, quite on their own, and when he leaned closer, she didn't know whether she had pulled him there. Her other hand reached back to steady herself against the shelf, and something about the way his breath hitched made her eyes close.

This close, Arden could smell the scent of her hair. Orange and jasmine – it went to his head as fast as the drink had. Before he could remember why he shouldn't, Arden reached out. Slid his hands from the dip of her waist to her hips, gripped the bones of her in his palms. He wondered whether Raven had always been so small, such a slip of a thing. Like a little bird. His fingers moved up the cool silver silk of her dress, over her the equally smooth exposed part of her back. He sucked in a breath through his teeth – she felt incredible. How did he not know she felt like this? He exhaled, and blew green anise over Raven's bare chest.

Raven's eyes popped open, and goosebumps prickled up under Arden's touch as she gasped. Why were his fingers burning up like this? She held on harder to the shelf and looked up at Arden, but his eyes weren't on her face. They were heavy-lidded and she watched his throat swallow as he gauged her reaction.

"Arden..." But she didn't have anything to follow it up with, just licked her suddenly dry lips and tried to remember what words were. Her thoughts swirled together, confused that Arden was touching her like this, confused that she liked it so much. There was a reason she shouldn't, but it just wasn't coming to her. Then his hands slid into her hair and her thoughts scattered again. The pads of his fingers felt delicious against her scalp, and he made a fist so her hair was pulled a little. The moonstones clinked softly together.

"You look so good like this," Arden whispered, his gaze moving down and back up but getting caught on her mouth. He leaned one hand on the shelf above her head, and dipped his head so that the tip of his nose ran from her shoulder to her throat. "Fuck, you smell so good, too."

Raven's hand curled in Arden's belt. He smelled good too – but she knew that already.

"You're just drunk," she mumbled. She fidgeted with the hem of his shirt, and his skin scalded her fingers. He shivered when she touched him, and something about having that effect on someone twice her size was some kind of intoxicating.

"Then I must have been drunk my whole life," he said, and

tilted her chin towards him.

"That would explain a lot," Raven tried to joke, but her hand was splayed against the flat of Arden's stomach now, under his shirt, and there was a strange electricity whispering over her skin.

"Big words for a little bird," Arden murmured, and if she hadn't been distracted by how sharp his teeth looked, she might have wondered why he had called her a bird.

Arden's hands cupped her face, long enough that his fingers slid into her hair again, and Raven leaned towards him. He had never looked at her like this before, and she was sure he could feel her pulse ratchet up where his palm laid against her neck. And now his thumb was moving along her lower lip.

"Arden," she tried again.

"Do you want me to stop?" he asked hoarsely, even as he pushed her further into the shelf. She shook her head 'no,' and the world faded to the hard line of his body all the way down hers.

"Then what?"

"I..." But again, nothing came. She gripped his collar, pressed up onto her tiptoes. Arden's yellow eyes glowed in the dim cellar, and she loved the low, rumbling growl that was sliding from his throat.

Somewhere in the back of her mind, a voice said, This is it. It's going to be you and Arden. This changes everything.

And the thought was as terrifying as it was wonderful.

At that moment, the cellar door banged open. Music and voices flooded in in a rush, like a wave of cold water. Arden let go of her, and whipped around with a vicious snarl.

"Sorry, sorry!" the partygoer said. "Just looking to top up the absinthe."

"Get the fuck out of here!" Arden shouted. The guest

scrabbled back up the stairs and the door closed again. It was quiet once more. Arden and Raven stood face to face, wide eyed for a minute.

Then drunken laughter burst out of them, and next thing they knew they were leaning on each other to keep themselves up right.

"Come on," Arden said, still laughing. "It's our birthday, this is for us."

He pulled the last green bottle off the shelf and took Raven's hand, leading her up and out of the cellar. Raven breathed in the cool air and her head cleared a little. She followed Arden out towards the lake, and they sat at the end of the pier and passed the bottle between them.

"Traditional faerie absinthe," Arden drawled. "That's not something you're going to find in your human town."

"Maybe not, but the whole point is to discover new and different things," Raven said. "There's a whole wide world out there, Arden."

"I'll drink to that," Arden said. He threw an arm around Raven's shoulders. The drink made them shameless, and they didn't have any further thoughts about what had happened in the cellar until the next morning, when Raven would wake to find herself panicking that they had ruined everything, and furious that she still didn't know what he tasted like.

Three

Yuletide

AS DECEMBER approached, Repanthe turned into a veritable winter wonderland. A human tradition, Christmas was the event of the year in the big city, and although it was not widely celebrated in Cressock, Raven had to admit she was dazzled. There were tinsel and lights wound round trees and lampposts all the way down the main street that led out to the harbour. Some of the smaller side streets had huge banners hung in rows, with giant red bows in the middle. Carts of roasted chestnuts and sugared almonds materialised on every corner, and cafes everywhere swapped black coffee for peppermint hot chocolate. In the courtyard in front of the old town hall, a Christmas market had sprung up. By the time the snow started falling, the sidewalks were all sparkling eyes and skipping steps. For the hard, unforgiving streets, and hard, unforgiving people, Repanthe was truly beautiful this time of year.

Raven had been recruited to the decorations team in the library. They said it was because of her 'creative flair', but Raven knew it was because her flying up to set up the top of the enormous Christmas tree was quicker and cheaper than setting up scaffolding. Nola and Dev came to keep her company. Dev had smuggled snacks in and was covertly feeding Raven, and Nola was poring through a book of fae lore that Raven had found her.

"So, are you guys going home for Christmas?" Dev asked. There was no doubting how he felt about the festive season. Christmas was still weeks away but he was wearing a sweater with a giant reindeer on it, and a headband that had mistletoe on top.

"Yes, but our family does Yule," Nola said.

"Same," said Raven, wrapping an empty box to go under the gargantuan tree.

"Right, of course. Do you know that in the human realm, there are several different end of year holidays, too. My dad says our ancestors, before the Realm War, had a festival of lights. But since we've been on this side, we do Christmas."

"Well in this realm, it's Yule all over, but different Folk have different ways of celebrating," Nola explained. "Some do two or three nights, some do all twelve. Of course, the uni only lets us off until New Year's Day because it's built around the human calendar."

"So, what does your family do?" He popped an almond into Raven's mouth while she struggled with a hefty length of ribbon.

"The tree nymphs do three days," Nola said. "One to give thanks to the forest, for it provides and nourishes. Two for Winter Solstice, when the Wild Hunt brings souls home to rest. Three for celebration, which is just the biggest damn party you've ever been to."

Raven met her eye and grinned. "Human Christmas is lovely, I'll give you that. But no one throws a party like a fae party."

"Damn straight," Nola said, pounding her fist on the table for emphasis.

"How about you, Raven?" Dev asked.

"Well, when we were younger, we did all twelve. My grandmother especially was very traditional. And a lot of the families still do twelve at home, but the whole town will do just two nights together. The Wild Hunt, and the after party."

Nola smacked her on the arm. "I'm sure your traditional grandmother would turn in her grave to hear you call it the 'after party'."

"What do you actually do for the Wild Hunt?" Dev asked. "Whenever I hear about it, people talk about dead people riding across the sky. Doesn't sound super festive."

Nola snorted. "Not quite. The Wild Hunt is a beautiful thing. It's about fear and horror, but also laying to rest and making way for new life. It's understanding and appreciating death as part of the circle of life. I honestly think it's why fae cope with death better than humans do."

"Yeah, we do not like to talk about death," Dev said.

"I'm sure there's something about the Wild Hunt in here…" Nola leafed through the book she was holding. "Okay, here we go."

She read out loud:

In the days when the Realm was young and the Faelings took their first steps, the Earth offered up rich bounties of feasting, and flowering, and favour. The Fae never slept, but danced in the sunshine and delighted in each other's arms by the light of the moon. They drank deeply from the providence of the Earth, their Mother, and filled the realm to the brimming. Soon, the Earth began to groan beneath them, and could not bear their weight. Warmth leached from the ground; the days grew colder, and the plants were not fit to eat. The Faelings, who had never been cold before, began to tire, and slow, until they laid their heads down on the Earth and began to slumber. Still, the Earth strained to hold them, and on the night of deepest cold, Odin heard the cry of the Mother. It was then that he mounted his horse of eight legs, and hurried to her aid.

When Odin beheld the sleeping Fae, his heart stretched out towards them. Some were hale and hardy, and dreamed terrible and fantastical dreams. But some had grown weak and were wasting away, and these had no dreams at all. Odin gathered these souls that were weary, and they were so thin he could carry multitudes in his arms. They woke at his touch, and tore their clothes to leave their lovers behind. But they were also glad, because the cold had touched their bones, and the will to dance had long left them.

And so they went with Odin, and he called them the Wraiths, they that were the first to depart the Earth. Then the days grew longer and the air warmer, and soon enough, life and breath returned to the lungs of the Mother. The Faelings flourished once more, although they had now found fear of the night, and closed their eyes to the darkness. The Mother rejoiced in the births of the fresh-faced era. But eventually these, too, grew heavy and the cold began to return. This time, the Fae were waiting for Odin. Those who had had their fill of life sat up through the night, and were received into the arms of the Wraiths. They did this so that their children would not starve, as the Wraiths had once starved. But, rather, they would drink in their share of the light and the warmth, and bear children of their own.

Since then, the Fae watch for Odin when the nights grow longer, and the night that he comes is the Solstice. The hunt is wild but the Mother is thankful, and Life is owing to Death.

Nola fell silent, and warmed with the rush of affection she felt for her kin. She had read voraciously through the fae literature online, as the university's database was quite extensive. But holding the old texts in her hands was deeply satisfying, and she intended to get to know the entire collection by the time she finished her course.

"That's really sad," Dev said.

"I think it's sad, but beautiful," said Raven. "My grandmother used to say that it's a good reminder that those of us who are left shouldn't squander our inheritance. And that's why we also have a giant party."

"That's the beauty of having both days," Nola added. "It fully acknowledges death and grief, but also life and celebration."

Dev nodded thoughtfully, toying with his red and white sleeves. "I can see that." He perked up. "But you still get presents, right?"

"Of course." Raven slid another gift under the tree. "And this year, I have somehow wrapped more decorative presents than real ones."

"Plenty of time," Nola said. "I make most of the gifts I give, because it's environmentally friendly. And also cheap."

"Well, I am not cheap, so I'll be buying my presents," Dev said. "Raven, why don't you come shopping with me this weekend? I can show you some darling boutiques in my area, they import from everywhere. Even the human realm."

"Sounds good, Dev."

Bright and early Saturday morning, Raven waited out the front of her townhouse, armed with a large empty bag and money from her extra hours in the library. Dev picked her up in the fanciest car she had ever been in, and she tried all the buttons and knobs.

"What does this one do?" she asked, for the thirtieth time.

"That's the seat warmer."

"Oh, my lord. There's a heater for your *butt*?"

"Toasty warm," Dev confirmed, wriggling in his seat in demonstration.

Raven laughed. "That is so human. You guys are crazy."

"Hey, it can really come in handy. It's getting super cold in the mornings. You've heard the phrase 'freezing your balls off' but you have you *lived* it?"

"I can't say that I have, Dev." *Seat warmers indeed.* She made a mental note to tell Arden about this.

They drove south out of the city centre and into the outskirts of the city, where Dev lived. The high-rises gave way to large, luxurious houses with green lawns in neat, perfect squares.

"Wow, this is where you live?" Raven said, looking out the window.

"Yep, this is why I still live with my parents," Dev said.

"So, where's your house?"

"Not too far from here. But I'm taking you to the mall. Seriously, you'll love it. This area is known for the shopping, and there are heaps of designer brands. But you'll also get really unique or rare items here."

Dev pulled up at a very tall building. It was smooth, dark grey, and shiny, relatively nondescript on the outside. But the inside was teeming with life. Every floor had a hole cut out of the centre, so that curling vines could fall from ceiling to floor, some ten storeys down. In the centre, an artificial waterfall collected over a graceful stone arrangement. The ceiling was painted like the sky at sunset, and as it sloped away from the central display, tiny twinkling lights shone brightly to provide warm, inviting lighting.

"So, the top floors are pretty much exclusive brands and utterly unaffordable. But downstairs is where all the treasures are." Dev took her down a lift, to the bottom floor. The elevator doors opened onto a much darker floor, with a closed ceiling. Below the water feature, then. The light seemed to be coming from orange lanterns, squashed into corners here and there. Without the roar of the waterfall, it was much quieter, too.

"Okay," Dev said, looking at his watch. "I will meet you back here at the elevator doors in two hours."

"We're not shopping together?" Raven asked.

"These are beautiful boutiques and they deserve your full time and appreciation. I, on the other hand, have a very specific and extensive gift list that ranges over eight floors of this building, to cater for sixteen adults and their associated offspring. We'll catch up after though and you can show me what you find."

"Big family, huh?"

"Oh yes. And I like to be efficient, so I'm trying to get everything on the one day. Time is money, et cetera." He tapped his watch. "Two hours." Dev spun on his heel and got back into the elevator they had come down, leaving Raven feeling slightly unprepared and unsure where to begin.

The first store Raven walked into sold the most amazing dresses. She found silk gowns designed to cling to waists and hips, huge tulle skirts that spilled out over the floor, heavy brocades of navy and gold like royalty. None, however, that accommodated wings, or tails, for that matter. Raven ran her hands over the fine fabrics, and they sighed at her touch.

The second store sold cut gems from all over the realm. Some she recognised, like the onyxes, moonstones, and opals. But some were precious stones from the human realm – rubies and emeralds that were clear like coloured glass. These were mostly out of her price range, but she managed to pick up a tiny, teardrop-shaped pendant that matched the colour of her mother's eyes.

The third store was a sweet shop. Raven bought a little of almost everything here: chocolates with assorted fillings, rainbow coloured jubes, fruit flavoured liquorice straps, jawbreakers the size of golf balls, individually wrapped lemon sherbets… the dusty candy store in Cressock had nothing on this place. She filled a large bag for her younger siblings to share, and a smaller bag of the especially wondrous treats for Arden: thousand flavour jellybeans, hard candies that were shaped into exquisitely detailed insects, crystalline rain drops that burst on your tongue.

By the time Raven had circled back around the elevator, she had also collected a mechanical sparrow for her father, an early edition book on chimera classification for Nola, and a small bottle of faerie absinthe for Dev. *Give him a taste of fae festivity,* she thought.

The last shop she stopped at was a perfumery. All three walls were lined floor to ceiling with glass bottles of all shapes and sizes and colours. Small placards helped to direct her: *Human Realm Hollywood, Florals and Nature, Vintage Fae,* they read. Raven spent some time in the section labelled *Unusual and Miscellaneous,* and found some surprisingly accurate scents including inkwell, old books, and freshly baked bread. Her favourites though were in the nature section – there was long grass, earth after rain, and sea spray. Best of all, was a plain green bottle that smelled of pine forests. It was a scent that always conjured home, and Arden, and it felt so intimate that Raven was suddenly glad Dev had left her alone. She purchased one and tucked it away in her coat pocket – a Yule present to herself.

The uni course wrapped up in a flurry of pop quizzes, last-minute essays, and one heated debate about whether it was politically correct to refer to chimera Folk as 'half human, half animal'. The professor encouraged them all to use their week off as an opportunity to get ahead on their assignments, but Raven was pretty sure he knew it was a lost cause.

In the last week, Raven, Nola and Dev were invited to a party hosted by a girl from their course. Her name was Melissa, and she had managed to pack a decent crowd into her campus-housing apartment. Raven and Nola were the only fae there.

Dev was in good form; he and Josh arrived wearing matching outfits. Nola looked stunning in a tight gold dress, and Raven was trying to be festive with glitter eye shadow. Melissa greeted them at the door then promptly disappeared back into the fray. The boys dissolved into the crowd soon after, leaving Nola and Raven stood by the trestle table of food.

"What… is this?" Raven said, holding up something red and cylindrical on a toothpick.

"I think, and I could be wrong here, but I believe that's some kind of cheap sausage."

"Right. There do seem to be a lot of processed meats here."

Nola made a face and put her cup down. "Wait till you try the punch. Or better yet, don't try the punch. Human parties are never worth it, I swear."

"Come on, we just got here. It might get better," Raven said, hopefully.

"Raven, have you ever been to a human party?"

"This would be my first."

"They tend to get drunker, but not necessarily better."

Raven laughed. "So, why did we come?"

Nola sighed. "I don't know, Dev seemed really keen and I guess I wanted to support him after what he told us about that shit with him and Josh. I didn't want him to get left alone if Josh decided to go off with someone else."

"Oh, that's so sweet of you."

"That's me," Nola said dryly. She took another sip of her drink without thinking, then grimaced and quickly set it down on the other side of the table.

"Hey, ladies!" Two guys sauntered up to them, one with terrible skin, and the other terrible teeth. "Enjoying the party?"

"Almost as much as the last human party," said Nola, bored.

The one with the teeth looked her up and down. "You're pretty for a fae thing. So, like, what are you?"

Nola stared at him.

"Let me guess," he said. "I'm usually pretty good at this. You're... a... kelpie?"

Raven prickled. "You do know that kelpies look like horses, right? You think Nola looks like a horse?"

The one with the skin leered at her. "Ooooh, you've got a lot of attitude for a faerie. Aren't you supposed to be like, delicate and feminine?"

"Do you want a feminine foot in your ass?" Nola said.

"Hey, we're just trying to make conversation here," said the one with the teeth.

"Yeah, why you gotta be such a bitch?" added the one with the skin.

"You have three seconds to fuck off, before I *show* you 'bitch'."

The two boys skulked away, and Nola glared after them.

"You're right," said Raven. "It isn't getting better."

"Come on," said Nola. "Let's get out of here."

"But what about Dev and Josh?"

"I'm pretty sure I just saw them sneak into that closet

together. I think they'll be fine."

Nola bought them both soft pretzels from a nearby street cart, and they strolled as they ate. It was a clear night, and the moon was full. The usually stately grey buildings winked with soft Christmas lights, pooling yellow on the slick cobblestones.

"So how long have you lived in Repanthe?" Raven asked Nola.

"Years," she replied. "I grew up not too far from here, and moved out when I was sixteen. Came straight to the city, got a job flipping burgers, and eventually went to nursing school."

"How come you moved out so young?"

Nola shrugged. "I don't get along that well with my family. I still go back every Yule though. They live in the forest just outside the city."

"I don't think I could have survived out here when I was sixteen," Raven said.

"You adjust," said Nola. "Not surviving is… not really an option. Like what are you going to do, lay down and die? You just have to keep moving forward. Same as what you're doing right now." She took a bite of her pretzel. "This is your first time living on your own, right?"

"Yeah," said Raven. "It's actually not as hard as I expected. I guess you're right, you just learn skills as the need arises. I miss home, though. And…" she thought about the café shooting when Arden had called her, terrified. "How did you feel safe in the city?"

"My first year out, I didn't want to sleep alone," Nola told her. "I thought someone was going to break in and attack me, after all the stories they told us about criminals in cities. And about how it's always worse for the Folk. So, I went tree-state all

82

night, because trees aren't as soft."

"Is tree-state like sleeping?"

"Not really. It's restful, but you don't dream, so you don't process emotions. You wake up stressed and sort of hung over. I was a zombie all year. Eventually, I was so exhausted that I didn't care any more, and I finally slept. Stayed asleep for like three days, and then I woke up and realised I was still safe in my bed. No one had tried to kill me in my sleep. My apartment was untouched. The door was still locked. And I've slept like a baby ever since.

"Plus, once I started nursing, I was so tired there wasn't much room to think about the fear. And then before I knew it, I was used to the city." She looked at Raven. "You're already doing much better than I was." Raven gave her a dubious look, but didn't argue.

"How did you get into nursing?" she asked.

Nola was silent for a time. Eventually, she said, "My older brother killed himself. I was fourteen, he was living here in the city. He came to visit us every few weeks, and seemed fine. Always laughing, always with stories from his exciting life. Then one day… he was gone. Left a note, apologising to my mother.

"As soon as I got the money together, I wanted to come out to where he had lived. Find out what all the fuss was about. And I've never left. I became a nurse so that maybe, just maybe, someone else would get to keep their brother. For a little while longer."

Raven exhaled. "I'm so sorry," she said.

"It's all right," Nola said. "Turns out, I really like my job. That's why I'm doing the trauma psychology course."

"That's a much better reason than me," said Raven. "I just did it to get out of my home town."

"That's a good reason, too," Nola said. "Becoming who you want to be is always a good reason."

A week later, it was the morning of the Solstice, and Raven was on the train back to Cressock. It was a six-hour journey so along with her duffel for the week, she had a smaller bag with a book, a comfy pair of headphones, and lots of snacks. Raven didn't mind the travel; it was a beautiful trip up. Black and grey cities melted into miniature villages, which, now that the snow had started to stick, looked like gingerbread from this distance. She had her book open in her lap but was staring out the window. She had gotten up when it was still dark, and now the sun was beginning to rise, painting the frosty landscape in delicate grapefruit colours.

"Mulled wine?"

Raven looked up at an old lady wearing a fluffy Santa hat, pushing a cart adorned with Christmas ornaments. A fat, silver pot sat on top of the cart, and in the bottom were rows of little mugs shaped like boots. Raven accepted a cup with thanks, and told the old lady to keep the change. She sat back and turned to her book, the mug warming her hands and filling the cabin with smells of cinnamon, orange peel, and cloves.

She had now been away from Cressock for over three months, and she was looking forward to the short trip home. She wasn't the only one who had left town as she grew up, although a decent proportion of Folk stayed their whole lives, too. As well as her family, Raven would get to catch up with a few other young fae who flocked back to the small village every December.

And then, of course, there was Arden. His recent visit to Repanthe seemed to make everything better, and worse. Better, because she was reassured to know they could still act like normal friends. Worse, because his physical presence after months apart had opened up a raw kind of missing him, an intrusive awareness of his not being there that worried at her nerves all the time. Raven had done her very best to ignore it, and for the most part, she felt like she succeeded. Her uni coursework had not suffered, nor her work at the library. As long as she kept busy, she was fine. But now the train sped her back to Arden, and her heart thumped in nervous anticipation. She worried that seeing him would make it worse again, that another separation would be awful. She worried that *not* seeing him would just kill her.

Sometime around midmorning, Raven fell asleep. She had always found travel soporific, and fell asleep often on trains and long car trips. She awoke to the announcement over loudspeaker that Cressock was the next stop, and that they would be arriving within the hour.

When Raven stepped off the train, the cold greeted her like the sharp claws of an over-eager pet. She had forgotten how much lower the temperature dropped out here than in Repanthe, and her breath huffed out in great white clouds. She smiled. Definitely home. Arden was waiting on the platform, and the sight of him standing there, hands in pockets, toothy grin, made her heart squeeze. She was so relieved to be seeing him there in real life, that once again her nervousness dropped away, just as it had the last time she had seen him. She ran at him, dropped her bags at his feet, and was lifted clear off the ground in a life-giving embrace.

In Arden's truck, Raven blew into her hands while the engine shivered to life and they waited for the fog on the windshield to clear. She shuffled along the bench to get closer to Arden; in his slouchy beanie and shearling coat he was the picture of winter warmth. Arden drove with one hand on the wheel, and his other arm slung around her shoulders. He chatted away about the housemates and his brother's latest antics, while Raven leaned into his side and breathed in the smell of him, until they pulled into her parents' driveway and Arden said, "Welcome home."

Knocking on the familiar front door, Raven felt simultaneously as if she had been away an age, and also as if she had never been gone at all. Her mother opened the door, all strawberry blonde ringlets and sea green eyes, and kissed Raven's cheeks.

"Hello darling, welcome back."

"Thanks, Mama."

Raven's mother was tall and slight, with much warmer colouring than Raven. She also had slender ram's horns that grew from just above her ears, that Raven could still yet inherit but wouldn't see for another ten years or so.

"Hi, Cecelia," Arden said behind her.

"Hi, love. Come on in you two, it's freezing out." She ushered them inside and took their coats, while Arden stamped the snow from his paws. The house was toasty, and smelled of burning Yule spices: juniper, cedar, and bay. Along the mantle, candles flickered merrily.

"Kids," she called. "Come say hello to Raven."

Three little faelings came bounding in, wrapping themselves around Raven's legs. She laughed in delight and picked up the youngest, Benji, settling him on her hip.

"Hey guys, I've missed you so much!" she said, touching their small heads. They were now eleven, eight, and three years old, and had all taken on their mother's fair hair, with only Raven being dark like her father.

"Raven, Raven," chanted the middle child. "Look at my

86

beautiful braids!"

Raven touched his short ginger plaits. "They're gorgeous, Nix."

"Thanks, Riley did them."

"Yeah, and Nix did mine," Riley said. Raven had to stifle her laugh – her tallest sister had her lovely curls bound up in wooden pegs and sticking out in all directions.

After Raven had sat with them all for an hour or so, she was left to unpack and settle in. Her father was a jeweller, and would be finishing work shortly. Arden went home, and Raven had a hot shower to wash off the day's travels. Finally, she sat in her childhood bedroom and began to prepare for the night's festivities.

Although the Yuletide celebration feast was the party of the year for any fae family, Raven had always liked the Solstice the best. She brushed a dark green shimmer over her eyelids and her lips. She slid silver rings over her fingers, one for every seven years of her life as was customary. This was the first time she had put the third one on, and she imagined Arden, at home, doing the same thing. Madeleine, the oldest faerie in the town, had stacks of countless rings and never took them off, her fingers so gnarled Raven wasn't sure if she could any more.

Like she did every year, Raven's mother came upstairs and sat with her, winding a wreath of mistletoe into her long, black hair. Cecelia always wore holly herself, braided by her husband Nicholas, but she liked the way the white berries stood out in Raven's hair. Then Raven did Riley's hair, and Riley did Nix's, and Nix put a pre-made holly crown on Benji's head while Nix was too young to braid and Benji too young to have much hair.

Raven glided down the stairs in her white Solstice dress, which had long sleeves and clung to her figure until it pooled on the floor. Her father, handsome with his jet-black hair and short, cropped beard, clasped her hands in his own and beamed at her.

"Wonderful to have you home, my love,' he said.

"Wonderful to be back, Papa." He kissed her fingers, and wrapped a heavy woollen shawl around her. Then took Cecelia's arm in his, and they led their family out to the town square, where the whole community was gathering around a roaring bonfire. Raven quickly found Arden and the Sliver clan, and the two families stood close by each other. Arden took Raven's hand firmly in his. He tucked a curl back behind her ear, and murmured, "You look lovely."

He wore his three silver rings on the middle three fingers of his left hand, and had mistletoe in his buttonhole. His eyes were melting topaz in the firelight.

The first ritual was the Burning. Everyone brought something of value to them, and threw it in the bonfire. This was to represent the early sacrifice to the Wild Hunt, the relinquishing of things that had been loved for make way for things that were yet to be grown. This year, Raven threw in some dried petals that she had saved from the flowers Arden had brought her. They had been pressed between the pages of the library's heaviest encyclopaedia, and she had not decided until about a week ago that she was going to give them up. She made sure Arden didn't see them though, embarrassed that she had been so sentimental.

The second ritual was the Humming. After placing your valued item in the bonfire, you were to light a candle from this fire. When everyone had taken their turn at the Burning, and the square was soaked with flickering light, the townsfolk would begin to hum. One by one until the thrum of it filled the frosty night air. It became one continuous, unbroken sound, as voices overlapped and blended. Under cover of this web, each fae would give private remembrance to those they had lost. As always, Raven thought of Arden's dad, and of her grandparents. This year, she also remembered Nola, and her brother's story. During this time, some fae would keen and cry. Others would laugh. All utterances were held within the steady collective breath of the community.

Once you had completed your remembrance, you blew out your candle. Faelings, who were mostly too young to have lost anyone yet, usually begun this process. This worked out well, since no one wanted to leave the young ones holding open flames too long. But the humming did not stop until every candle was extinguished, and there were certainly some who had long memories. It could take over an hour for all the lights to go out, but fae did not rush grief and thanksgiving.

Finally, the third ritual was the Darkness. After all the candles were out, you kissed the faces of those you loved the best, once on each cheek. Then you had to make it home safe before midnight, when the Wild Hunt would pass over and collect the lost souls, and any who were caught out on Solstice night. Raven kissed her parents, her three little siblings, and Arden. One two, one two. One two one two one two. One, two. Those she loved the best.

The next day was the Yule Festival, and the winter sun beamed down at them in delight. The Lightfoots woke early and had breakfast together, then exchanged gifts. Cecelia gave Raven a small stack of books, the kids had gathered her a dreamy bouquet of wildflowers and mushrooms. Nicholas had made the most beautiful necklace, a black sapphire laid in silver filigree, set on a black velvet band.

"For my raven-haired beauty," he said, "the midnight colour

that binds us."

He helped her with the clasp behind her neck, and then hugged her tightly.

Then they went door knocking to exchange gifts with neighbours, but this was increasingly difficult as the morning wore on. The whole town was a flurry of activity; Folk zipped around stringing up brightly coloured bunting, lanterns, and garlands of flowers in every open space. Petals drifted softly towards the cobblestones, and scented the chilly air. Tables were dragged out into the town square in place of the bonfire, in rows from one end to the other, and every family laid food down for the communal feast until the tables groaned and threatened to buckle. Musicians in thick furs parked themselves around the square, and had offers of wine and fresh fruit juice throughout the day, so they never thirsted. By the afternoon, everyone was there. But where the previous night had them standing solemnly in rows, on this day, life burst forth from all over. Faeries perched on balconies and rooftops, fluttering their wings for balance. The sound of hooves rang out as fawns and satyrs danced over the flagstones. Faelings ran back and forth, with ribbons streaming from their hair. And everywhere, laughter tumbled and gambolled amongst them.

Raven chased her siblings around, danced with her father, and brought plates of food to the fiddlers by the fountain. A school friend caught her up and spun her around, gleefully.

"Little Raven Lightfoot," she said happily.

"Elodie! How are you?"

"I'm excellent, I'm *engaged.*" She held out her wrist, and showed off the gold bow tied around it.

"Congratulations! Who could the lucky man possibly be?"

"None other than local hottie Marlowe Twofinger, of

course!" She leaned in conspiratorially. "It's a *shotgun* wedding too, because I'm *pregnant!*" Elodie grabbed Raven's hands and jumped up and down, her lovely long hare ears bouncing along with her. Raven laughed and leapt about too, delighting in her friend's joy. It was hardly a scandal; Elodie and Marlowe had been together since they were thirteen and had always talked about the big family they were going to have one day. Through their high school years, they ran their parents ragged with worry, sneaking out of their beds most nights and threatening to start said family prematurely. Raven imagined it was a great relief to everyone that Elodie and Marlowe had managed to graduate before the first pregnancy. They moved in together the second they were out of school, and now ran a graphic design company from their kitchen.

"And how are you, how's Repanthe city?" Elodie asked, when they had settled.

"I'm good, Repanthe is hectic."

"I'm sure," Elodie said. "Is it mostly human, like they say?"

"Oh yes, very much so. You could walk around all day and not see another fae."

"That's wild." Elodie got a mischievous gleam in her eye. "And what are human *men* like?"

"Ugh. Awful," Raven said. "I only went out with one but it didn't end well. And then they told me that that's just normal over there, so I didn't see the point in trying again."

"Aw, Raven, I'm sorry to hear that. You're sure it's not worth giving them another chance?"

"Look I'm sure there are nice men out there, but honestly, it doesn't seem worth it. I went to the city to study and learn about myself, not to find a man."

Elodie nodded. "That sounds fair. Although... I've known

you a long time. You used to get upset if you weren't hugged enough, if I recall," Elodie said.

Raven made a face. "I secretly still do. But you know what, the course I'm doing right now is fantastic. Study will just have to be my boyfriend for now."

"Oh, yes. Trauma psychology. The angst, oh the angst."

"All right," Raven teased, "just because *you're* loved up and have your life sorted…"

Elodie laughed and held up her hands. "Sorry, sorry. You're right. It sounds like an important and fascinating topic, and I think you could really make a difference out there. I've always believed in you, lady." She nudged Raven in the ribs. "But if you get sick of the sob stories, you can always come home and we'll find you a nice fae boy."

Elodie stood and headed off to go meet up with Marlowe. Before she left, she gave Raven a long, tight hug. "One for the road," she said in her ear.

As the sun set and the temperature dipped, coats and scarves were hauled out, along with tall gas heaters. But the festivities would not slow until the small hours of the next morning. Raven went round the square, catching up with old friends, and trying home-brewed meads and moonshines. Arden found her later that night, sitting by the fountain to rest for a minute.

"How are you doing?" he said, handing her a tall glass of water.

Raven squinted at him with one eye shut. "Very full of food. A little tipsy. Super happy." She grinned up at him. "You?"

"Pretty similar. But approaching my quota of Folk for the day. You want to take a walk?"

"Sure. But you gotta pull me up."

Arden hauled Raven to her feet, and she swayed on the spot.

"Turns out I'm also really tired," Raven said.

Arden rolled his eyes. "You want a piggy-back?"

"Yes!"

This was a time-honoured tradition that started when they were nine, and Arden decided that the best way for him to build muscles on his skinny boy-arms was to run around with Raven on his back. Raven had no strong feelings on the body-building component, but had loved being carried around like royalty. As they got older, he did it less often, but throughout their teenage years was known to carry her around if she asked very nicely when she was drunk, or not feeling well, or exceptionally tired.

Arden carried her away from the noise of the huge party, and padded into the woods. Raven inhaled the pine smell, and it was every bit as good as she had been remembering these last few months. Arden's un-tameable hair brushed against her chin as she bobbed with his gait.

The forest was no mystery to Raven and Arden. Their whole childhood they had escaped into the trees, adventuring among the benevolent boughs. They knew the paths inside and out, knew where the fae beasts made nests, and what time of year was most dangerous. Midwinter, although darker and colder than the rest of the year, was also when the beasts slept the most deeply.

Arden set Raven down but took her hand, and they picked their way through the mushroom circles.

"So, is it weird being back?" Arden asked her.

Raven shook her head. "Not at all. You know how much I love Yuletide; I wouldn't have missed it for the world. It doesn't feel like I'm here on holiday, it's more like the other way around. Like I just went for a short trip and now I'm back home and it's over."

"You *are* home," Arden said.

"I know, but I live in Repanthe now. So, technically, that's my home. Or, at least it's my house. Still can't believe I live there, to be honest."

"Do you like living there?" He held a branch out of their way.

"I think so. It's satisfying living on my own and feeling like I'm thriving. I mean, I think I'm thriving, it's only been a few months so I suppose that's too short a time to really tell."

"Didn't feel that short to me," Arden said. There was quiet for a while. Then, "Are you happy to be back here?"

"Of course," Raven replied.

"And…" Arden said more slowly. "Are you happy to see me?"

Raven stopped walking, and Arden, still holding her hand, was pulled up short. She touched his face, but he didn't meet her eyes. "Of course," she repeated.

He looked at her then, and there was a sudden sadness in his expression.

"What's wrong?" she asked.

Arden toyed with a lock of her hair. "I didn't think it would be this hard," he said.

Raven brushed snow off his ear. "Me neither."

Arden settled his arms around her. "I've wanted you back all day."

"I've been here."

"I don't like sharing you."

Raven smiled. She hadn't heard that in a long time. When they were faelings, Arden used to say it all the time, and adults had to remind him that he couldn't prevent other children from playing with her. Raven didn't tolerate his jealousy either, and he soon learned that if tried too hard to keep her she would slip straight through his grasp and into the sandbox with another kid.

"I thought you grew out of that," Raven said accusingly.

"I'm relapsing," he mumbled into her hair. He sighed, and his breath sent shivers down Raven's spine. "Sorry, are you cold out here?" he said. He opened up his coat and wrapped Raven inside it. She slid her arms round him gladly. He always did run hot.

"I find it hard to be away from you too," she said to his chest. "But I—"

"I know, I know," Arden interrupted. "You have to find out who you are on your own, and so on. I'm not asking you to come back. I'm just saying it hurts."

"I'm sorry I'm hurting you," Raven said quietly.

"It's okay," Arden said. "But I kind of want to know something."

"Mmm?"

Arden was silent. Raven pulled her head back and looked at him.

"Let's walk a little further. The midnight flowers will be out soon."

"Arden, what did you want to ask me?"

"Give me a second. It's hard to say out loud."

Raven quirked an eyebrow, but was silent and let him pull her along. They wandered on until they reached a huge fallen tree, nearly as tall as Raven even on its side. Arden dusted the snow off a section of it, lifted Raven easily up onto the trunk, and then pulled himself up to sit beside her. Raven waited.

"Brutal honesty?" Arden asked. Raven nodded. Arden huffed out a cloud of cold air, and spoke to the trees. "I always thought that someday, you and I would end up together."

Raven was quiet with shock. She didn't know what to say to

that, but it certainly wasn't what she was expecting. Not after he had brushed off The Incident. It was somehow both what she most wanted and most dreaded to hear.

"I mean I know we're twenty-one and it's too early for us to 'end up' anywhere. And I never pushed because I figured, you know, we have so much time and it'll happen when it's meant to happen. But then at our party that thing in the cellar happened and…"

"You remember that?" Raven asked, shocked.

Arden barked out a laugh. "Of course. I had frustrating dreams about it for a week."

"Then why didn't we ever talk about it?"

Arden shrugged. "What was the point? You were going off to Repanthe and you were so excited about it. I wasn't about to get in the way of that."

"But you could have said—"

"Said what, exactly? I'd never ask you not to go. And while we're being honest, you could have said something, too."

He had a point there. Arden swung a leg over the tree to face her.

"And I thought, okay, it's not what she wants right now. Maybe everyone's right, maybe some distance will do us some good. At the end of the day, I'm not some slobbering teenager coming after you, we're best friends. I'm going to want whatever makes you happy, with me or not.

"But, fuck, Raven, all I could think about is how you were going off to start a life far away, and I never actually kissed you that night. I just have to know. Did you want me to?"

Raven broke under his searching, amber eyes. "Yes," she whispered. "Yes, of course I did."

Some emotion Raven couldn't read flickered over Arden's

face. He reached out and took her face in his calloused hands, while his molten stare flared and turned hungry.

"And," he began, pausing to swallow. He looked at her mouth instead of her eyes as he spoke. "Do you still want me to?"

Raven's heart beat so hard she was sure Arden could hear it.

"Arden, I'm leaving at the end of the week…"

"I don't care." She watched the jump in his jaw.

"If anything happened here, I'd still have to go."

"I know." Arden leaned his forehead against hers.

"It's a bad idea," she breathed.

"That's not what I asked. I asked if you—"

"Yes." The word slipped out before she could catch it. "Yes, I still do, I still…"

And then Arden was tilting his head to slide his nose down her nose and the words got stuck in her throat and her heart roared in her ears and then he was pressing the softest kiss to her lips.

Raven's eyes nearly flew open for the shock of the feeling. Her blood turned to lemonade, full of sugar and sherbet and sunshine. The taste of him crackled in her mouth, and the squeeze of his hands at her waist jolted up to her throat.

Arden pulled back and dipped his head, still close enough that his hair tickled her nose. He was breathing hard.

"I… uh," he paused, and then looked up at her. His yellow eyes glowed. "Is that… how this normally feels to you?"

Raven shook her head. "Definitely not."

He gave her a lopsided grin. "Me neither."

Arden slid a hand around the back of her neck, and pulled her gently back towards him. As soon as his lips touched hers, the bubbles surged up through her veins once again. Arden seemed to react the same way, kissing her more deeply with a distant sound slipping from his throat, and suddenly she wanted to drink him in like he was air. Her hands grabbed fistfuls of his jacket, and his arms wrapped tightly around her so his fingertips brushed her ribcage.

"Is this okay?" Arden breathed. Raven just nodded, and touched her nose to his. He slid his hands up under her hair, loose curls falling from her thick braid, and kissed her again. It was sweet wine, and oak, and wood smoke in his mouth.

And the sharp edge to it all, the thought this might be the only time Raven would have this, only made everything the sweeter for it. She pressed into the heat of his body, and tried to soak him into her bones.

Then Arden's tongue touched hers and set off a whole new chain of sparks down her spine.

"So, this is what you feel like," he said muzzily. "You feel so breakable."

He kissed her again, long and slow this time. Raven shivered against him, fizz pooling in her stomach, and he gripped her tighter. She could feel his heart beating against her sternum, his teeth gently clamping down on her lip.

"Not that breakable," Raven said. Arden grinned, his canines gleaming white and sharp in the dark.

"Oh yeah?" He rose fluidly and tipped her onto her back against the tree trunk, trapping her with his lanky limbs so she didn't fall off the side. A deep growl rumbled from somewhere in his chest as he kissed her again, rougher than before. His tongue licked at hers, and their teeth clicked softly together.

"Still not that breakable," Raven murmured.

Arden chuckled, and laid a little of his weight on her. After months and miles of separation, it wasn't enough. She pressed closer, grabbed at his shirt, and bit at his lips. It was only a minute longer that his caution held. He shuddered, and let his full weight press the air from her lungs. Good– kissing Arden was better than breathing. She exhaled into his mouth, and wrapped her arms around his neck.

"See?" she whispered, and felt his lips curve against hers. He didn't reply, only let their tongues slide and their hands tangle and their hips kiss until Raven's head was spinning and her fingers dug into his ribs.

Arden leaned onto his forearms, either side of her face, and she breathed in again. He moved down and sucked at the hollow of her throat.

"Maybe I'm the fragile one," he said onto her skin. "I fall apart when you're not here."

Raven closed her eyes, as his lips started trailing under her jaw. "You've never fallen apart in your life," she told him. "You're the strongest person I know."

Arden brushed his lips back up over her chin, nipping her lower lip, and then pulled her up to sitting opposite him. He held her small face in his hands, and stroked his thumbs over her cheekbones.

"You're wrong about that," he said quietly. He kissed her lips, then her knuckles on both hands, and sighed against her fingers.

Around them, the midnight flowers suddenly bloomed to life. Hundreds of little white blossoms opened and offered up their glowing hearts, petals that had come off here and there drifting up towards the night sky.

"Glad Jul, Raven," Arden said. *Happy Yule.*

Four

Pushes and Pulls

THE PAIR drifted slowly back into town, where their absence had gone unnoticed and revellers were far from tiring. Raven, on the other hand, was wilting fast. She leaned on Arden as they walked, and he slid an arm around her waist to support her.

"Do you want me to take you home?" he asked against her hair.

No, Raven thought. She wanted to spend all night with him, wherever he was, preferably without anyone else. But she also wanted to make it out of Cressock at the end of the week. So, she said nothing, just smiled, looped her arm through his and let her big lug of a best friend walk her home.

They reached the Lightfoots' front door. Laughter and music wafted in on the breeze, but as Arden stepped in close to Raven, everything fell away. He kissed her forehead, her nose, her mouth.

"Does this feel weird, for you?" he asked her. She shook her head.

"No. It feels like we've always done this."

Arden nodded his satisfaction, then nipped her lip.

"I know you're not staying," he said. "But if it's this hard for me, I'm going to make it hard for you, too." He flashed a wicked smile, before cupping her face in his hand and catching her earlobe with his teeth.

"Don't be mean to me," Raven said, closing her eyes as his tongue flicked over the corner of her jaw.

"I'm just reminding you of reasons to come back." He kissed her again, sucking her bottom lip into his mouth.

"And what if I don't want to come back?" Raven struggled to get the words out.

Arden pulled away, and for a moment, his luminous eyes were shot with pain. He stroked his thumb down her cheek, and over her lips. Then he smiled and said, "Then we'll just have to have a very good week this week."

He reached for her again, but she pulled back.

"Wait. Not too good a week, Arden," she said. "You have to give me *some* chance at leaving here intact." When he looked at her blankly, she clarified, "Just... moving slow, all right?"

He gave a frustrated sigh. "Okay. I get it." He took her in his arms again. "I hope you'll change your mind, but I'll make sure you're the one calling the shots."

She put her arms up around his neck. "So you'll go easy on me?"

Arden grinned his most wolfish grin. "Not a chance." He lifted her off her feet and kissed her long and sweet until her bones were jelly, then set her back down.

"Goodnight, Lightfoot," he said, and then loped away into the darkness.

The next day, Raven woke up with the taste of Arden on her lips. She slipped quietly into the shower before anyone else had awoken, and wondered what it all meant. On the one hand, she was happy. Deliriously happy, as she touched her fingers to her mouth and felt the echo of the lemonade fizz he had left there, *finally* answering the unspoken question of their September

101

birthday.

And that first kiss... the memory of it seemed almost unreal as it smoothed itself across the backs of her eyelids. She shook her head. There was just the small matter of her still needing to go back to Repanthe and him staying here. The matter of all the things she had done so far to avoid a life married off and stuck in Cressock. Some part of her felt horrendously guilty at having slipped up, of starting something with Arden that she couldn't finish. Was it her responsibility to be gentle on his feelings, or was it his choice to engage in something he knew couldn't last? How much was she actually allowed to enjoy this?

Raven hadn't come up with any answers when the water suddenly ran cold. She gasped and hurriedly shut the tap off, scrambling for her towel. Someone must be in the kitchen with the water on.

For the rest of the day, Raven shoved the issue aside and focused on being with her family. She was determined not to brood during this wonderful time of year.

The kids had written a play to put on for her, and Raven applauded until her hands hurt. She helped her mother fix the car, and then went down to spend a couple of hours in her father's studio. She carved a little wax ring, like she used to do for hours while waiting for Nicholas to finish work. Raven found that conversation with Nicholas always flowed best when his hands were busy, so they sat and worked together as he filled her in on local gossip.

"Now *don't* tell your mother I told you," he said, "but she's in a tremendous fight with one of the Harkaway mums two doors down." Nicholas loved gossip.

"No, the Harkaways?" Raven responded, suitably shocked. "But we went over there and delivered Yule presents yesterday morning!"

"I know," said her father. "You wouldn't know it, they always play nice in public, and you know your mother would just hate it if Folk knew there was drama brewing." He looked down and inspected the gold piece he was polishing, turning it back and forth. "Truth is, they haven't been on speaking terms in over a week."

"But Mama loves the Harkaways," Raven said.

"That she does," Nicholas replied. "But she loves Riley more, and it came around that Indigo Harkaway has been harassing our Riley at school."

"Tut tut, Indigo."

"Indeed. So, Cecelia marched over there and tried to get the Harkaways to apologise. Well. Of course, Yana tried to smooth things over but Leonore says it's *Riley* who's the bully, and says *Cecelia* should apologise." He switched the head of his polishing tool, and restarted the machine.

"So, what does Riley say?"

"Riley couldn't care less! She and Indigo made up almost immediately and have been thick as thieves. Their main complaint is the difficulty of their mothers!"

Raven laughed and stared fondly at her father, his eyes twinkling and his moustache twitching. He was Cressock down to his bones.

That night, Arden came over for dinner. It was Raven who opened the door, and became a little breathless at the sight of him.

"Hi," was all she said as he stood in the doorway.

"Hi yourself," Arden returned softly.

"Come in," she invited him, but neither of them moved. She had seen him on this stoop a hundred thousand times, but somehow this time she couldn't remember what to do with herself. Arden gave a low chuckle, and brushed his fingers over her waist. For a second, she thought he might kiss her, but then he stepped around her and into the house.

"Just be normal, you freak," Raven muttered to herself, and followed him into the dining room.

Arden sat with his flannel shirt sleeves rolled up to the elbow, revealing the shonky tattoos on his left arm that he got right after their eighteenth birthday. He hadn't told his mother beforehand, and she didn't speak to him for a week. Raven sat down in her usual place beside him, and took a heavy plate of potatoes from her father as he bustled in and out of the kitchen with last minute touches.

Arden was a well-established figure in the Lightfoot household, and the two younger boys climbed all over him. Despite Raven's earlier jitters, Arden was the picture of ease, lifting Nix and Benji in to the air, and joking and gently teasing Riley. But all night, his thigh pressed up against Raven's, and every so often, he would lean back in his chair and swiftly stroke his fingers down Raven's back between her wings. She felt it all the way up and down her spine. Raven leaned into him like a magnet, and had to keep reminding herself to sit up straight in her chair.

"I was wondering," Arden said after dinner, "if I could steal Raven away for a night."

Raven raised an eyebrow. "Steal Raven away for what?" she said.

"Well, I know she only has a few more days in Cressock," he went on, still addressing her parents, "but the guys are planning on taking a little camping trip in the mountains. Before everyone has to go back to work."

"Well, I think that sounds like a wonderful idea, Arden,"

Cecelia said.

"Difficult time of year for it, no?" said Nicholas.

"It's cold, sure," Arden replied, "but we're all young, invincible, and off work." He grinned, and Nicolas laughed.

"Fair enough. What do you think, Raven?"

Under the table, Arden squeezed her knee. He looked across at her, and his eyes were rich, melting butter.

"I think it sounds perfect," she said.

Early the next morning, Raven arrived at the lake house. There were five housemates including Arden: Jade with the mohawk, sweet and adorable Sadie, and water sprite twins Liza and Alexis. She knocked on the door, and Sadie opened it.

"Raven!" she squealed, throwing her arms around her.

"Hey, Sadie," she said, hugging the plump little fawn back. "Good to see you."

"And you, my darling." Sadie kissed both her cheeks, and led her inside.

Liza and Alexis were sitting at the kitchen table, arguing over a map, and Jade was perched on the bench top. She greeted them all, and added her pack to the pile in the hallway.

"Raven," Alexis said. "Tell Liza that the path through Scornway's Pass is faster than going over Hickory Ridge."

"I *know* it is," Liza said to her brother through ground teeth. "I'm saying that Hickory Ridge is slower but a better view."

"Hickory Ridge is a great view," Raven said. "But, honestly, I don't think we'll have time to make it that way round before nightfall. At least not in winter."

"Ha!" said Alexis, putting his feet up on the table.

"But," Raven said quickly, "we could probably come home that way if we leave at dawn tomorrow."

Liza grudgingly agreed, and Sadie swatted Alexis' boots off the table.

"I think it's a great plan," enthused Jade, who was just happy to be included.

Shortly, Arden's heavy paws could be heard clumping down the stairs.

"Raven, is that you?" he called. His head popped around the doorway.

"Hey Arden. Are we heading off soon?"

"Soon," he promised. "Come up real quick, I want to show what things look like now that you've been gone a while."

Raven followed him back up the stairs, past her old room that was now Jade's. It felt strange not to automatically head that way. She ducked into Arden's bedroom instead, where it was warm and smelled like him.

"What's new, it looks pretty much the same to me…"

Arden pushed her back against the door so it clicked shut, the wood cool against her wings.

"Nothing," he said against her throat. "I just wanted to get you alone for a second." He put his hands on either side of her face, and hovered his lips over hers. "We'll join the others in a minute." He smiled, then kissed her softly.

The lemonade bubbles immediately reappeared, fast and fizzy as they had been in the woods. Arden's face was rough with stubble, but his lips were soft and full. His hands slid into her hair as he crushed her to him again. Raven breathed in as Arden breathed out, and was pushed back into the door again with a small thud. He smoothed his hands over her hips, then lifted her up against the wood, causing her wings to pop out slightly.

"I thought I was calling the shots," she gasped, as her hands ran over his shoulders.

"Tell me to stop," Arden said, starting to kiss his way down her neck.

"I…" she struggled.

"Yes?" Arden ran his nose back up her throat, and kissed just under her ear.

Raven gave in. "Don't stop," she said on an exhale.

Arden stroked down the backs of her thighs, and hitched her legs up around his waist. "Yes ma'am," he said, and rolled his hips against her with a groan. He kissed her mouth again, this time all teeth and tongue. He felt so good against her, Raven thought she could swallow him whole. She tangled her fingers in his silver-grey hair, and kissed him again.

Arden growled deep in his chest, and Raven felt the vibrations of in her bones. He lifted her from under her legs, and carried her to his bed. She was laid down on worn-in cotton covers, and immediately pulled him back to her. He laced his fingers through hers, lifted her arms above her head, and kissed her sweet and slow. Drowning her in molasses.

His hands still holding hers, Arden ducked his head down and moved the hem of her shirt up with his teeth, to press hot, wet kisses up her stomach and in the hollow of her ribcage. Raven caught a glimpse of his tail flicking through the air, before her eyes slid closed. Her breath started to shallow, and she tried to reach down to him but his hands held her firm.

"You're not going anywhere," he said under her ear.

Harsh banging on the door made both of them jump.

"Let's go kids, we're burning daylight!"

Arden snarled and shot daggers at the disembodied voice beyond the timber. Raven, still underneath him, giggled.

"We'd better get going," she said. Her eyes were bright in the dim room.

Arden put his shaggy head down on her chest, and his big wolf ears smudged her chin. He got up, very reluctantly, and pulled her off the bed. Raven brushed a piece of lint from his hair, and Arden straightened her shirt. He opened the door, but just as she was walking out, he grabbed her by the waist and murmured against her temple, "You look very sexy rolling out of my bed."

He stepped past her and trotted down the stairs, leaving Raven to follow, kiss-dizzy and holding the banister as she went.

The air outside was crisp and wonderful. The cold breeze was much appreciated on Raven's clammy skin, still recovering from being rolled in Arden's bed. The six of them crammed into Arden's truck, with Raven riding shotgun, and they drove for the mountains. It only took an hour so reach the start of the trails, then they would have a five-hour hike to get to the campsite. Big backpacks had never sat well over Raven's wings; she usually carried bags with a shoulder strap, but the ache was well worth it for the clean country air. Raven wanted to bottle it and take it back to the city with her.

They stopped for lunch, Sadie distributing sandwiches and juice boxes. Then they were on the move again, and reached the campsite with a good amount of time before sunset. Liza grumbled under her breath that they could have come up through Hickory Ridge.

"There's maybe an hour left before dark," Alexis argued. "We'd need at least two to get over the ridge."

Everyone else told them to shut up.

There were three tents between the six of them, and they had planned to set up so Sadie and Raven were in one, Jade and Arden in another, and the twins in the third. Arden started making up a campfire, Alexis and Liza went to get more firewood to last the night, and Jade fetched water from the nearby stream. Sadie began preparations for dinner, and Raven set a couple of rabbit traps. They worked easily and companionably, having gone on many camping trips like this one while they all lived together. Jade, who had only recently moved in, was new to the gang and keen to prove her worth. She ran back and forth, bringing up more water than the six of them would use in a night.

After darkness fell, and bellies were full, they all sat around the fire and passed around a bottle of spiced wine that Sadie had thoughtfully packed. Alexis plucked away on a battered guitar, singing softly to himself, and Raven leaned against Arden contentedly.

"What's the city like, Raven?" Jade said.

Raven sighed. She had been asked this so many times in the few days she had been home. For a while, she had been keen to talk about how exciting it all was, for Folk to be proud of her for moving up in the world. But in this moment, she didn't particularly want to go back.

"It's crowded," she said, "but I think everyone is lonely." Arden stroked slow circles into her lower back.

"It's beautiful, but it stinks of iron all the time." She sighed and closed her eyes. "It's so, so big, and pretty much anything you can think of is available for purchase somewhere. But people walk around buying up stuff like they can't find the thing they're actually looking for. And they're living in one of the oldest cities in the Realm but no one knows about the fae that lived there before them."

No one said anything for the while, and the fire cracked and popped noisily.

"So will you go back?" Liza asked eventually.

Raven opened her eyes. "Yes, I'm going back at the end of

the week."

Liza looked mystified, but she didn't probe any further.

"I'm thinking about moving down to the city," Alexis said. Liza stared at him.

"Since when?" she demanded.

Alexis shrugged. "I don't know. It's boring here."

"But what would you do?"

"I don't know, Liza!" he said exasperatedly. "What do I even do here?" He settled back and struck up a new song on the guitar. "Maybe I'll take this with me and make some music."

Liza snorted. "You're going to be a starving artist?"

Alexis shrugged again, and didn't take the bait.

"Well, I'm staying," Sadie said decidedly. "I just couldn't imagine leaving here. Away from everyone I know and love, out there all alone…"

Alexis looked up. "You never get bored here?"

Sadie shook her head. "I've never really needed that much excitement. I'm home more than the rest of you, and perfectly fine with it. Cressock is small enough that it's homey, but big enough that we've got everything we need right here."

Liza nodded her agreement. "I'd consider moving to maybe Tulloch, or even the Morrow. But no further in."

Alexis shook his head. "Then you may as well stay in Cressock."

"What about you, Arden?" Liza said.

Arden stared into the fire.

"I'm comfortable for now," was all he said.

Liza decided to change the subject, and asked Jade to tell them a campfire story. Jade, eager to impress, launched into a terrible tale of how, when she was fifteen, she had stolen her father's car to see her girlfriend in the neighbouring town, only to drive straight past her dad on her way home and watch him waving his fist in the rear-view mirror.

When the fire had died down, everyone got up to perform their bed time rituals and ablutions. Raven crawled into the little tent, shivering now that she had left the fireside, and huddled down into her sleeping bag. She was in there alone for about five minutes, unable to get warm, when Arden's bulky frame squeezed itself in next to her.

"Move over, Lightfoot."

"Arden? What are you doing here? Where's Sadie?"

Arden settled himself in next to her, shirt unbuttoned and beanie gone. He pulled her into the curve of his body, trying to stop her shivering.

"Sadie's in Alexis' tent tonight," he said.

"Then where's Liza?"

"Liza is with Jade, and I am with you," he explained. He unzipped her sleeping bag and pulled it out from under her, causing her to roll into him. Then he laid it out like a blanket over the two of them instead. She thought to protest, but the warmth of him seeped to her bones and her teeth finally stopped chattering.

"Okay, well that last part I noticed," she said. "What, so everyone is sleeping with everyone now?"

"Welcome to small-town life," Arden said dryly. "There's not a whole lot to do out here."

"Then why didn't they just pair off in the first place?"

Arden shrugged. "For some reason, they like to pretend they're sneaking around and nobody knows. I guess we're still in high school. Sadie went to Alexis and Liza's tent and suggested Liza spend some quality time with you before you go back to Repanthe. So, Liza got up, but came straight to our tent and said

111

she had something really important to discuss with Jade and sent me out to you. She also asked me not to tell Sadie I had come here."

"Okay, I think I followed that?"

"Honestly, I barely followed it. I don't care, I'm happy to be here." He rolled her over to face away from him, then snuggled into her back and stuck his face into her shoulder. "You smell much better than Jade," he said. The brush of his ears against her neck sent a completely different kind of shiver through her.

"A gremlin and a water sprite, huh? That's not something you hear often. Gremlins hate getting wet."

Arden snorted a laugh. "I think she'll make an exception."

"And Sadie and Alexis? Alexis is so grumpy, I wouldn't have thought she'd go for that."

"I think he's secretly sweet to her when no one's looking." He slid a hand under her shirt and stroked lazy circles into her stomach. The warmth felt amazing, and his fingers on her abdomen made her both more and less relaxed.

"So, what now, is everyone going to up and musical tents again in the morning?"

"God, I hope not," he said. "I'm not getting into Liza and Jade's sex tent."

"Right, so we all just do a mini walk of shame tomorrow."

"I guess. I really couldn't care less what they do." His fingernails scratched at her belly lightly, and she had to fight to keep thoughts in her head.

"And they're going to think we're sleeping together, too," Raven said.

"Again," Arden mumbled, "I really couldn't care less about them."

He rubbed down the outside of her thigh, his hand hot even

through her tights.

"Are you warm enough?" he asked. He pressed his lips to the back of her neck, and folded his large hands over hers. "Your hands are still cold."

"I'm fine," she said. "You're like a giant hot water bottle." But she rolled around to face him, and she laid her hands on the dark red-gold skin of his broad chest. He lifted her chin, and put his mouth on hers.

Heat flooded through Raven's body, much more efficient than any sleeping bag. A growl rumbled in Arden's throat, and every time Raven thought they were going to break apart, he just caught her tongue again and brought her back to him.

"Why does kissing you make me feel like I'm on crack?" Arden mumbled.

He rolled over, pushing her onto her back and bracing himself on his forearms above her. Their hips slid against each other, and she hooked her fingers into his belt loops.

"I don't know," Raven replied, her breathing hitching. "How would you know what being on crack feels like?"

He pushed his knee between her thighs to move them apart, and the feel of him pressing up against her had her eyes rolling back into her head.

"I don't," he admitted, "but if it's as good as this I'd give it a go."

Arden's rough hands pushed her shirt up, so that they had skin contact down the front of their bodies. She could feel the heavy muscles of him, so incredibly warm, and arched up to get closer. His fingers floated down her side, and slid into the waistband of her tights. Some small part of her brain waved a white flag.

"Arden," she said between kisses.

"Mmm,"

"This is dangerous territory," she said.

"Why's that?" he asked, his lips moving down her collarbone.

"I'm trying very hard not to sleep with you," she said.

"Why are you doing that again?"

"You know why."

Arden sighed and rolled them to the side. He slid his hand up her back under her shirt, and started massaging the back of her neck.

"Something about leaving here in one piece," he said, repeating her earlier reasoning. His fingers moved slowly back and forth, making her mind slide in and out of clarity.

"That's right," she said, although she was already starting to regret it.

"I remember," he said. He rolled her back over to face away from him, and slid forward against her back. He was so much taller than her; she felt completely surrounded by him.

"You let me know, Lightfoot," he said, scraping his teeth across the top of her shoulder. "If one day you don't need to be in one piece. You say the word, and I'll tear you apart."

By the end of the week, Raven was wrung out. She had seen a lot of old friends, and done some shopping for fae clothing that cost three times as much in the city. But every day, Arden had found time to catch her alone, and get his strong, calloused hands on her skin. She would feel drunk on the taste of him, and every time she met his butterscotch eyes, she would feel like she was falling until she could touch him. As the days went by, it got worse and worse. She could barely stand to be in a room with him without some kind of contact. If there were Folk around, she would content herself with holding his hand and inhaling the forest and earth smell of him. If they were alone, she felt like she had to work to keep her clothes from falling apart at the seams. The strangest part was, it didn't feel sudden or awkward between the two of them. It felt like he had always touched her this way, like he couldn't be more familiar.

At the end of the week, it was Arden who drove her back to the train station. He thought about driving her all the way home, but it was just delaying the inevitable. Halfway there, Arden pulled over and kissed her so hard her lips felt bruised afterward. And then, finally, they stood on the platform, holding tightly on to each other, with nothing left to say.

"Take care of you," Arden whispered to her. He kissed her on each eyelid, then on the lips.

"Take care of you, too," Raven said back, and breathed in a final lungful of Arden, and of home. He stood outside so she could wave to him out the window as the train pulled away, and before she knew it, he was gone again.

The trip back to Repanthe was much bleaker than the magical journey out. It seemed that the colours slowly leached out of the landscape as they sped along, so that by the time Raven got off the train, she was back in the ashen tones of the iron-boned city. The smell burned in her nostrils and settled over her skin uncomfortably, worse for having grown unaccustomed to it with time away.

But as she walked home from the train station and the streets became more familiar, Raven found she did not mind the anonymity in the gentle flow of the crowd. After being asked so many times why she was returning to the city that she began to lose belief in her answers, it was sort of peaceful, knowing that no one would stop her or try to talk to her. Besides, she felt the matronly buildings nodding to her as she turned onto her street, and that was welcome home enough.

Raven got back to her little town house, put the kettle on, and got the fire going. Then she sunk into her squashy armchair, and closed her eyes. The tangled truth was, leaving Cressock again was hard, but she was actually starting to feel at home – if not in Repanthe as a whole, at least in this tiny house that she had made for herself. Because there was no one else living here, the place was so *her*, and that was something she'd never been able to explore in a town where everyone had a version of her they knew and expected her to be. So, while she had been sad to leave, she also felt a kind of relief to be back in her own patchy lounge room.

Leaving Arden... that was worse. But that had to be something she sealed off inside herself, because it threatened to overwhelm everything else. If they did end up together, Raven wanted to know that they were whole by themselves first. And that Arden got to be everything he wanted to be, outside of them. She loved him. But they had never been Elodie and Marlowe, and she didn't want to be. So, she packaged it up tightly and locked it away.

Raven showered with her back to the hot water and her forehead on the cold wall tiles, then fell into bed and slept fitfully, dreaming that Arden was there with her and then waking up freezing cold.

The next day, Raven dragged herself to class. The morning was blanketed in a thick mist, the buildings blackened in the grey light and beheaded by the fog. The cobblestones were slippery under her boots.

Raven didn't particularly feel like studying that day, but she was keen to see Nola and Dev. She also hoped that reengaging with the course material would renew her sense of purpose in being here. She met Nola for coffee before class started.

"Hello, darling," Nola said, as Raven sat opposite her. "How was your Yule trip?"

"It was perfect," Raven said ruefully.

Nola nodded. "It's hard to come back the first time. It gets easier."

Raven looked down at the mug she was cradling. "I kissed Arden," she confessed to her coffee.

If Nola was surprised, she didn't show it. "And what was that like?"

Raven lifted her eyes to Nola's, and was suddenly glad that it was Nola with her and not Dev. For all that she thought the world of him, she didn't want him to fuss and celebrate and ask why they weren't together.

"It was also perfect," she confessed. "But it didn't change anything. I still want to be here, it's just a bit harder to remember why." She made a face. "And it made me remember that I really miss physical contact."

"Did he try to get you to stay?" Nola asked.

"No, actually, he was so good about it. I don't know if that makes it better or worse. I feel like such an asshole."

"That's a good thing," Nola assured her. "I'm glad he didn't put pressure on you. And you're not an asshole for making life decisions outside of a man."

"But I didn't have to get involved with him and make it harder for him."

"He's a big boy, it was his choice to get involved too. Use it as motivation to have a meaningful life here. Know that you made a good decision and did not give him up for no reason."

"How do I do that?"

Nola shrugged. "That you'll have to figure out yourself. But I do have an idea for a starting point. My hospital is looking for someone to be a fae health worker. I think you should apply."

"Am I even qualified for that?"

"After this course, you will be. The role is not about being medically trained, it's about giving our fae patients someone who will be there for them in a sea of humans. And advocating for what they need, when the human team doesn't even know how to think about that."

Raven shook her head. "I don't think I know enough to do that."

"I think you'd be surprised. It's a very intuitive thing. It's also only three days a week, so it'd be a good taster of the industry. Think about it."

"Okay," Raven said, "I'll think about it."

"That's my girl," Nola said.

Over the next few months, Raven doubled down on the reasons she had to stay in the city, and shoved down the awful feeling that maybe leaving Cressock made her cold and selfish. The days got warmer and longer, but she spent a lot of time indoors in the library, either working or reading in the fae section for her final uni presentation. Arden called a few times, but she pushed him off with excuses about being busy with studies. She became so invested in her topic that she ended up speaking to the professor about extending her post grad certificate into a diploma, and taking on another six months when the current course was over. Raven also applied for the job at Nola's hospital.

"Why do you want to work at the Repanthe City Hospital?"

Raven took a breath before she answered. "Because I came to the city to do something worthwhile. And I think your fae patients are worthwhile."

Nola was waiting for her outside the interview room, and when Raven stepped out thirty minutes later, Nola wrapped her arms around her. Raven was offered the position on the condition that she pass her course.

The night before the presentations were due, Raven practiced her speech in front of Nola and Dev. She had asked if they wanted to take turns, but Nola said she wasn't worried, and Dev said he was too worried to get through it more than once. So, she stood nervously in front of her two friends, and tried not to read too much off of her palm cards. In the end, it wasn't as difficult as she thought: the topic was something that meant a lot to her, and turns out she could speak about it for as long as people would listen.

"Not only are fae patients more likely to leave hospital early if they even make it in there in the first place," she told them, "it is often their being fae that makes them sick in the first place. The Folk are greatly over-represented in statistics regarding suicide, mental illness, and being victims of violent crime. They also have higher rates of major diseases, particularly the closer you get to the city, combined with less resources to get treatment.

"When you have adverse experiences on a day-to-day basis, as many fae do, your cortisol levels ride at a high level for extended periods of time. This has major impacts on your mental health, like chronic anxiety and stress, as well as your physical health, like blood pressure, hearth health, and digestion. What this means is that trauma, including experiences of discrimination, actually makes you sick."

When she finished her presentation, Nola applauded her

loudly. Dev applauded too, and offered to make her a soundtrack from his band.

"The band is still going?" Nola asked incredulously.

"Yeah, and we're getting a lot better," Dev said earnestly.

"With that… fringe girl from the club?"

Dev made a face. "God, no. Josh's cousin Drew stepped in. He's high most of the time but a decent singer. And he promised he'd start showing up to practice once his bail is posted."

Nola shot a look at Raven and said nothing.

"I, uh, think I'll go classic and not use a soundtrack," Raven said. "Thanks for offering, though."

Arden texted her that night.

Good luck for tomorrow, you've got this.

She had sent him a copy of the presentation to look over, with a twinge of guilt for still relying on him. She could have as easily sent it to Nola. He had sent an email back saying, *Super proud.*

When the semester ended, Raven had a week off before starting her position at the hospital. She put in all her paperwork to extend to the diploma, and scrubbed her house from top to bottom in a fit of spring cleaning. Being such a tiny house, this did not take long. She fondly recalled the brownies at her high school, and felt that the janitorial staff at the university were not quite the same. She finally spent a day in the spring sunshine, stretching out her wings. She got her results back from the course, and was satisfied with the outcome. And then, when she eventually ran out of things to do in procrastination, she picked up the phone and called Arden.

Since leaving Cressock, Raven had been determined that her brief entanglement with her childhood best friend would not be the downfall of her adult life in Repanthe. So, she had been nervous about what their friendship would be like after they had parted ways. She told him that her phone camera was broken in order to avoid video chatting with him, and mostly tried to restrict herself to text messages rather than phone calls.

Picking up on the hint, Arden had started calling less, and he put in an impressive amount of effort into remaining cheery and supportive of her despite his background worry that he had pushed her too far over Yuletide. At first, he felt the pain of her second departure so sharply that he was glad she didn't immediately reach out. But, over time, he began to miss her, sorely, and she was not coming back to him. So, when Raven made one of her rare phone calls to him, they both had news.

"Hey, Lightfoot."

Arden's voice made Raven's heart squeeze uncomfortably.

"Hey, Sliver. How are you?"

"I'm good. It's good to hear your voice."

She hugged a pillow to her chest. "It's good to hear yours."

"I hear congratulations are in order, you've got a fancy job."

"Oh, thanks. How did you hear?"

"Cecelia told me." There was a short silence, and neither of them brought up the fact that Arden had never had to get news through Raven's mother before.

"So, tell me about it, what will you be doing?"

Raven switched the phone to her other ear, and thought about how Arden always had his phone on speaker because phones were not designed for wolf ears. A million little things she knew about him.

"It's kind of patient support role, I think," she said.

"You think? They didn't tell you what you'd be doing?"

"Well, it sounds like a lot of the role is actually up to me. I'm supposed to be there for fae patients at the hospital, and help the medical team work with them. So, I guess they can't tell me exactly how to do that."

"Well that sounds like something you'd be great at," Arden said. "Folk always feel better when you're around."

Raven laughed. "I don't know about that," she said. "I don't think I've made a particular difference to anyone."

"I think you'd be surprised, Lightfoot."

"Thanks, Arden."

Arden hesitated, then said, "Actually, there's something that I've been wanting to tell you, too."

"Oh yeah?"

"Yeah. I'm, ah, moving out of Cressock."

Raven nearly dropped the phone. "You're what?"

"Yeah. I've signed on to a project out at West Bay, building houses in really rural fae communities."

"Arden, that's amazing. I can't believe you're leaving Cressock."

"Neither can I, to be honest," he said. "But I've been thinking a lot about all that stuff you've been going on about. You know, being our own fae and doing meaningful things. And I figured I'd give it a go, too."

"I think that's incredible. I'm really proud of you."

Arden laughed. "Thanks, kid. I'm proud of you, too. There's uh, one other thing. West Bay is really far out. They said we probably won't get much reception or internet out there. We're all being given radio devices to communicate on the ground. But other than that, it'll probably be only once a month or so that we travel out towards the nearest major town for supplies. So, you might not hear from me for a while."

"Oh," Raven said.

"Yeah. But I just wanted to say before I go," he pushed on, "I really hope I didn't fuck us up. You know, last time you were in Cressock. I don't know when we'll get a chance to really talk again, but I didn't want to leave it unsaid. I'm sorry if I pushed you too hard."

"No, Arden, don't apologise." Raven suddenly regretted the distance she had enforced between them. "It wasn't that you pushed too hard, I... I had an amazing time with you."

"Me too," he said. "I was worried maybe you thought it was weird, after you had some time to think about it."

"It wasn't weird. Actually, it felt so completely natural, with you."

"For me, too." Another pause.

"It's just..." Raven began. "I guess I'm being selfish. I wanted to have you but also my own separate life. And I didn't want it to hurt so much, even though I knew it would hurt you more."

"Don't apologise," Arden said. "You don't owe me anything. I just want to know we're okay."

"We're always okay. Promise."

"That's good. And... I want you to know that I really do want you to do this solo life you're trying to do. So, when I move to West Bay, I thought..." Arden took a deep breath. "I thought, I'll do that too. And I don't want you to have to think that you have to, like, wait for me or anything. Not that I expect you have been. But I mean, after what happened with us, I want you to know I don't have any expectations."

"Oh," was all Raven said.

"So, ah, go ahead and see other people, if that's what you want." He let out a harsh sounding laugh. "For all I know you already are, I just assumed because I'm not. That sounds so awkward, I'm not doing a very good job of this. It's just, no pressure, you know? I can't say I'm letting you live your life but then also tie you to me."

Raven's throat felt like it was closing up. "Thanks, Arden." Then she added, "You know it's not because I don't want you, right?"

"I know, Raven."

"And I'm not seeing anyone either."

They sat in silence for a moment.

"When do you leave?" Raven asked.

"Couple of days."

"How's your family taking it?"

"Well, actually. I told Asher that he was going to be in charge while I was gone, and he's really taken it on board. He's helping Mum at home, he's working with Lachlan in the shop… should have left him ages ago."

"Colour me impressed," Raven said.

"The boy might have hope yet."

They lapsed into silence again.

"All right, I'd better go," Arden said.

"Okay." An anxiety flooded her that this would be the last time she would speak to him for a long time, but for the life of her couldn't think of anything else to say.

"I will always love you, Raven." Her heart broke.

"I'll always love you, too, Arden."

"I know. I'll speak to you in a couple of months."

And then he hung up the phone.

Five

Summer

THE SUMMER rolled in thick and heavy over Repanthe city, settling in like smog. Raven opened all the windows in her little house, but the humidity clung stubbornly to the walls and wouldn't let up. Raven's bedroom, on the second floor of the townhouse, was a sweaty nightmare, despite the standing fan she had picked up. Downstairs was slightly cooler, but with only the armchair in the living room, she couldn't exactly sleep down there.

Raven was glad, then, to be at the hospital three days a week. Repanthe City Hospital was a sprawling white complex to the east of the city centre, about a half hour walk from the university and some distance from the main road. There was a direct bus from near her house, but on her first day, Raven went by foot.

She walked past a row of enormous apartment blocks, new-looking with squares of glinting glass like a hundred sharp edged eyes. There was something mesmerising about the dizzying height of them, dark charcoal to match the rest of the city, stark against the washed-out blue of the sky. After a way, Raven had to look away for the crick starting in her neck from staring upward.

The road to the hospital was especially smooth, lest an ambulance find a pothole on its critical journey. In contrast to the centuries-old cobblestone still lining the walkways in the middle of the city, Raven's footsteps were soundless on the black asphalt here. The hospital complex itself was immaculate. On the far side, the private wing had a glittering granite face, and its own small lawn. In the front, the public hospital had sandstone benches and great wide doors that blew perfectly conditioned air out when they slid automatically open. Nothing but the best for the best and richest hospital in the country.

Inside the main building, there was lush blue carpeting and many silently gliding escalators. To the right, there was a tidy reception desk with a smiling human lady behind it. To the left, a cafe with potted plants suspended in little rope baskets. For a place where you went in emergencies or disaster, it was certainly a tranquil greeting. Maybe that's why the emergency department was round the side.

Raven did not see Nola on her first day. Nola, having finished her post grad certificate, was back to full time work and was on night shift the week Raven started. Regardless, Raven would have to get to know the whole hospital and not just the mental health wards where Nola worked.

Raven learned that she was working in a team with two other fae, and she was the youngest of the three. There was a middle-aged fire sprite, who wore thick glasses and had smoke curling from his head at most times. He had to wear a special cap so as not to set off the alarms. And there an ancient-looking dwarf who had been working in the hospital twice as long as Raven had been alive. The dwarf told her how he had had to fight for the position, and was only allowed to stay when they realised too many fae were dying for reasons the human medical team did not understand. Raven had been shocked at some of his stories, but even more shocked to learn that some of the doctors missed even the most basic fae health information. Irritating, then, that many of the doctors acted like she did not exist.

During her first couple of weeks, Raven went to see patients with one of the other fae workers. Raven was told it was easier for some of them to speak to a non-human, particularly those with living memories of the Realm War and the painful periods of human settlement after it. Mostly, they sat and kept fae patients company in the whirlwind of human faces and unfriendly-looking monitors.

One morning, after she had started to work independently, Raven arrived at the ward to see a rusalka with a broken arm. She had first met her the Friday prior, and was fond of her. She reminded Raven of her old landlady. The medical team had just left and were deep in discussion around the corner.

"Good morning, Mrs Rushing," she said. "How are you this morning, can I plump up those pillows for you?"

Mrs Rushing looked pale and tired. She had awful bags under her eyes, and her lips looked cracked and painful. She smiled and nodded to Raven, leaning forward. Raven reached around her, and frowned. The old rusalka's hair was damp, but the pillows were almost dry.

"You can't be comfortable like this, have you told a nurse your sheets are drying out?" Raven asked.

"I've been trying and trying, but they won't let me have wet bedding," she said. "I've been using the water bottles but they only give me one or two a day."

Raven marched around to the team. "Excuse me," she said politely. "I've just noticed that Mrs Rushing's bedding is drying out. Can we get some water on her pillows please?"

The doctor frowned. "We don't want her to get cold, she can't sit in a wet bed – it puts her immune system at risk. And she's already developing a fever."

Raven gaped at him. "She's a *rusalka*. If she's getting sicker it's because she's drying out."

"I can get you some water," a nurse said. The doctor waved her off.

"I don't care what she is. I won't have a febrile patient of mine lying in soaking sheets."

"Right, well, I'm telling you right now that if you don't wet her down, she'll die," Raven snapped. "So, I'm going to do that so your patient will survive, and we can argue about it when you're not killing her."

Raven stalked away, still fuming, picked up several water bottles from the nursing station and emptied them over Mrs Rushing's pillows and around her head. She brought a basin over, filled it at the sink and then dipped the old fae's long hair into it, using her hands to scoop the water up over the top of her head. She sighed, and closed her eyes.

"Thank you, dear."

It wasn't until a moment later, when she was sitting and combing the rusalka's hair, that she realised she had just run her mouth off at a junior doctor. It wasn't like her to get confrontational. *Oh well,* Raven thought. *What else was I supposed to do, let her get sicker and sicker?*

Sure enough, after about thirty minutes, her colour started to look better, and the bags under her eyes lightened. A nurse came over and confirmed that her temperature was coming down, too. Raven left Mrs Rushing to rest, and gave the nurses instructions on how to keep her hair and pillows wet. She made a note to come back later and make sure a doctor didn't step in and dry her out again. Any guilt she had about being rude dissolved and was replaced by a sense of deep satisfaction. She prepared a more level-headed speech about why she went directly against a doctor's orders, but no one came to reprimand her. No one came to thank her or apologise, either.

Another day, she sat by a young goblin's bedside while the medical team spoke to his parents. They had flown into Repanthe to get a consult, because there were fewer treatment options in some of the rural towns. The goblin child had never been around so many humans, and was nervous to be left alone. At first, Raven didn't feel very helpful – goblin culture was something she knew less about than most other fae, as they tended to live in the rocky mountain areas in the south and not near Cressock. But the parents later thanked her for coming, and said she made the environment feel a little safer just for being there. She noticed as well that when the couple spoke to the team, they mainly addressed their questions to her, even though a human doctor was giving the information.

"So, we've booked the scan for Friday," the doctor said.

"Ah, we thought we'd only have to be here 'til Swiftak," the goblin's mother said to Raven.

"I'm so sorry," Raven said, "Grimstak is the earliest he'll be able to get in. Is it possible for you to stay one more night? I could talk to the social worker if you need a place to stay."

The doctor looked annoyed, but didn't say anything.

Some fae didn't want to see her at all, and that was okay, too. There were one or two instances where fae had come in with longstanding conditions, and said they didn't care who was there as long as they got their treatment. Some had just grown up in Repanthe and didn't feel out of place or in need or particular support.

In her first couple of weeks, Raven wanted nothing more than to pick up the phone and tell Arden everything. About the ignorance of the human treating teams, about the rudeness of the doctors, about the satisfaction of sometimes getting to help someone. But then she would remember that he was in West Bay, and unreachable. A few times, she dialled just in case, and sure enough got sent straight to voicemail.

"Hey Arden," she said to his mailbox. "I know you won't get this for a while. I just wanted to call and hear your voice. I have so many hospital stories for you when you can get through." She paused. "I hope everything's going well out there. I haven't heard from you in ages but your mum says she got your letter in the mail so I take it that means you're alive out there." She laughed but it came out brittle. She rushed on.

"Anyway, I'm sure you're doing amazing things out there. Can't wait to hear about it when you're able to call me. I'm proud of you, but I'm also missing—"

There was a clipped beep and the recording cut her off. Raven sighed. Arden had warned her it might be a month until he could get in contact, but now three months had gone by, and still nothing. But Raven couldn't be annoyed at him − after all, she was the one who wanted space.

The post-grad diploma was a continuation of what Raven had been studying in her certificate, and she was still very much enjoying the content. But without Nola and Dev, class was significantly less fun. Now, there were no fae at all in her class, and sometimes the discussion would turn to issues regarding colonisation or fae culture and heads would swivel in her direction expectantly. Raven was torn between wanting to set the record straight, and being frustrated that she was singled out like some kind of display specimen.

"I wish you were still there with me," Raven said to Nola one afternoon over lunch, when they found themselves on the same hospital shift. Raven had visited a very old faerie in Nola's ward, who had had terrible flashbacks of fleeing the Seelie Court as a little girl. She became near catatonic in the presence of the human doctors.

"I didn't feel alone with you in class," Raven added.

"I'm sorry, chicken," Nola said. "Come out with me and Kofi tonight, we're going to that new pizza place on Crescent Street."

"I thought you were double dating with Dev and the new boy? Brian?"

Dev had broken up with Josh at the end of their course, and had been dating a string of new people since then. He didn't talk much about it, but did loudly lament the untimely death of their band.

"He and Brian split up," Nola sighed. "He's actually on a date with someone else tonight. Matt something."

"*Another* one? I think that's the third Matt he's gone out with. Why is every human boy called Matt?" Raven said. Nola shrugged.

"Don't ask me why humans anything," she said. Raven picked at her sandwich.

"Where does he even find these people?"

"The internet, where does anyone find anyone?"

Raven rolled her eyes. Dating apps were big in the city – in fact, Dev said they were the only way to meet people these days. But, coming from a small town, the whole process seemed unnatural to Raven, and she didn't find it surprising that Dev had difficulty finding lasting romance on an app called *Heat*.

To be fair to Dev, though, Raven remembered that she hadn't exactly had much dating success in real life either. The other week she had walked past Elias at the university, and recalled with distaste that he had talked about doing his PhD there. She had thrown her hair over her shoulder hurried on, as if hiding her face would disguise her when she was also the only one for miles around sporting giant wings. She feared that if he saw her, she'd have to talk to him. Or worse – that he'd see her, and not remember her at all.

"So, will you come?" Nola's question snapped her back to the present.

"Sure, Nola, sounds good."

Raven and Dev had met Nola's human boyfriend a few weeks ago. He was huge for a human, with big shoulders and long legs. He had umber coloured skin and short dreadlocks.

And he looked at his tree nymph like she was his own personal Eden.

"How's the job going, Raven?" Kofi asked over pizza. He had a rolling, deep voice.

"She's fucking killing it," Nola jumped in. "The other day she gave it to a doctor who didn't know how to treat a rusalka patient."

Raven blushed. "You heard about that? You weren't on that shift."

"Yeah, but Ariella was, and she told everyone." Ariella was another one of the handful of fae nurses at the hospital. "So badass," she added. "I knew you'd be great at this job."

"I've never really told anyone off like that," Raven admitted. "I just couldn't believe this guy was going to let a rusalka go without water because he thought he knew better."

"Good job standing up to a doctor, too," Kofi said.

"Honestly, I don't think I thought about who it was," Raven said. "It was just some guy in the way of this woman getting the care she needed. Actually, I think it's worse that it was a doctor, because he could overrule someone who maybe wasn't as sure as I was."

"Exactly," Nola said with her mouth full. "I told you that you would be more than qualified."

"But that hasn't exactly been reassuring," Raven countered. "I keep being surprised at what they don't know. Don't they have some kind of unit on fae health at medical school?"

"They do, but it's very short. And even then, it's just not something they practice every day, so they forget it," Nola said.

"I'm glad you're there, then," Kofi commented. "Imagine what goes on when there isn't a fae worker available."

"There often isn't, so I'm honestly trying not to," Raven said wryly.

"They die," Nola said bluntly. "They get shit care in human hospitals, and die of treatable conditions. It's not a mystery, it's a historically documented and yet largely ignored fact. Which is why you," here she pointed at Raven with her pizza slice, "are invaluable."

"Sounds like a lot of pressure," said Kofi. Nola had picked the olives off her pizza, and Kofi was loading them onto his own slice. "How do you manage?"

"I guess I hadn't thought about it like that. I mean, I'm really happy to help out when I can. And I've got some pretty supportive friends, like Nola."

Nola rolled her eyes. "Raven, name me one friend you have that isn't me or Dev."

"Hey," Raven defensively. "I have plenty of friends."

"*In Repanthe*," Nola clarified.

Raven opened her mouth, then closed it. She looked over at Kofi, but Nola caught her.

"Kofi does not count as one of your friends."

"Aw come on Kofi, you like me, right?" Raven said to him.

Kofi shrugged, and sipped his drink. "I mean I don't know you very well. But yeah, I like you."

"See?" Nola said accusingly. "I thought if you started working at the hospital you'd leave your shitty library job and develop a social life."

"My library job is not shitty," Raven argued, tearing apart some garlic bread in her fingers. "And I can't quite pay my rent on three days a week."

"Okay, that's fair, but you're in there almost every single day."

"I study!" Raven protested.

"You hide," Nola countered. She softened. "Ray, I know it's been hard to come back from Cressock. I think you are kicking ass at work, but Kofi's right. If you want to keep being awesome, it might be good to make sure you're doing something for you, too. Self-care, and all that shit."

Raven sighed. "Okay, so what do you want me to do?"

"I don't know, what do you like doing?"

"I genuinely like being in the library," she said. Nola rolled her eyes.

"Okay, you're a giant nerd and you clearly haven't gotten around the city enough yet."

Kofi clicked his fingers. "I know what we can do!" He got a wicked gleam in his dark eyes. "It's a bit naughty, so I think it will satisfy Nola's criteria. But it's still within Raven's interests."

Nola looked at him sceptically. "What are you thinking?"

"We break into the library!" Kofi looked around triumphantly, but the girls just stared blankly back at him. He tried again. "Okay, give me a chance. I have a friend who also works at the library, and he says there's a secret stash of really old booze in there."

Raven shook her head. "Who's your friend, I'm pretty sure I'd know if there was secret alcohol in the library."

Kofi grinned, his teeth perfectly white in his dark face. "Oh, you wouldn't know Isaac. He works in the archives."

Raven frowned. "But nobody goes into the archives, we use an automated system to search the old stock…" Her eyes grew wide with realisation. "You mean there's actual people working down there?"

Kofi looked smug. "There sure are. Not many, but Isaac does and he knows more university secrets than the dean herself."

Nola nodded. "Yep. This sounds perfect."

One coffee later, they were sneaking through the campus grounds like thieves. Raven felt a bit ridiculous, because actually there were still lights on in buildings. Being in the city centre, and the hub of education and arts, there was always something going on at the uni – theatre kids rehearsing, night owls putting study hours in, maintenance staff hard at work… the library itself was actually open until eight at night most days, although Raven worked day shifts. She glanced at her phone. It was half past nine.

They followed Kofi around the side of the building to a small hatch Raven had never noticed. He tapped three times on the rusted metal doors, and after a minute or so, they creaked open and a shaved head popped through.

"Hey, guys," the head said.

Nola reached out and shook his hand. "You must be Isaac," she said.

"Yeah, that's me. You must be Nola. Which makes you Raven." He turned his head and winked at her. Isaac had pale, white skin, wide eyes, and sharp-looking cheekbones. His ear lobes had been pierced and stretched to hold hollow silver circles.

"Hey," Raven greeted him. "How are you still here this late?"

"I never leave, I live in the library," Isaac deadpanned. Then he broke into a grin a second later. "Just kidding," he said. "Kofi texted me you were on your way and I snuck in. Come on through."

He disappeared back down through the hatch, followed by Kofi and Nola. Raven wrinkled her nose as she let herself down – the rusty flakes gave off a strong iron odour. Nola coughed and waved them out of her face, but didn't comment.

Isaac led them through a claustrophobic but thankfully short tunnel, and opened a door. They came out in a room Raven had never seen before. She supposed this was the archives. The ceiling was low but the room was enormous, appearing to stretch the entire floor of the library without any wall breaks. Rows and rows of shelves stretched wall to wall, ceiling to floor. Now that they were inside, it no longer smelled of iron, just a little musty. The air was drier and cooler than outside had been.

"Welcome to the archives," Isaac said as he walked, his arms outstretched and his head turned to look over his shoulder at them. He was wearing a stretched out old black jumper that hung off his tall, lean frame, and black jeans full of holes. His silhouette reminded Raven of a large bat. They traipsed down the corridor the shelves had created, and walked past endless amounts of books,

"So, you guys actually have to comb through all those books to find whatever it is we put in the search tool?" Raven asked.

Isaac laughed. "What did you think, we had robots to do it?"

"Something like that," Raven admitted. "Everything in the city seems to be automated. And the books always come back so fast."

Isaac puffed up proudly. "Yes, well, we keep impeccable systems down there."

"We?" Raven queried.

Isaac tapped the side of his nose with a long, thin finger. "Secrets," he said.

They reached a small office attached to the wall. It had brown, wooden walls, and a door with a glass pane in it. Isaac reached into the room, and came out bearing two dusty bottles.

"These are also secrets," he said with great relish. "But these kinds of secrets, like all the best ones, are for sharing. Come on." He led them to a small staircase and another door. This door took them into the main level of the library, where Raven was suddenly on familiar grounds again.

The library at night looked completely different. With so many little reading nooks and closely stacked shelves, the shadows were very dark and deep. But when they popped out into the central study space, Raven felt like she was in another world altogether.

The moonlight streamed in through the stained-glass window, and where rainbow hues usually splashed out over the tables, there were only eerie tones of blue and green. Everything was bathed in this cold, muted light, and Isaac suddenly looked a lot less human and a lot more like her. It was then that she noticed that his ears, while not as pronounced as hers or Nola's, were slightly pointed at the top.

Raven found some glasses left over from the library Christmas party, and they poured out the wine between them. In the blue light it looked inky black, which Raven felt was fitting as they were sat in the library among all the books. The wine was strong, and delicious, tasting of faintly of blackberry.

Nola and Kofi picked up one of the bottles and wandered off

to explore the library, but Raven, knowing the building well already, was content to sit against the window. After a steaming hot day, the cool glass felt good against her skin.

"So, what brings you to the big city, little faerie?" Isaac asked her.

"How did you know I was new?" Raven replied.

Isaac shrugged. "I've seen you around the library, I know you're new here."

"I haven't seen you."

He grinned. "No one sees me."

"Are you fae?"

"Half. My mother was."

"Ah." She sipped her drink, and Isaac poured her a little more.

"So, what brought you here?" he repeated.

Raven shrugged. "Something about being independent and learning about myself," she said. "I don't really know any more."

"Do you regret coming?"

"No." She smiled into her cup. "Sometimes I'm grumpy about it, but I feel a lot more useful here than I ever did in Cressock. Like I'm finally good for something."

"That's awfully honest for someone talking to a guy they just met," Isaac said conversationally. "It's probably stuff like that that gives you away."

Raven shoved him on the arm. "I thought honesty was good," she said.

"Yeah, when you're five and your mother asks who broke the cookie jar," Isaac retorted. "When you're an adult in the city, you're supposed to play it a bit cooler than that."

"Well, I clearly have no idea how to play it cool," Raven said.

"First," Isaac said, "drink more." He poured more wine into her glass.

"You know it's difficult to get fae drunk," Raven said. "We have a pretty good tolerance, because we usually have stronger drinks."

"Well," Isaac said, filling his own glass. "I am half fae. And my other half has just had a lot of practice. So come on, keep up with me." He clinked his glass against hers, and drank off half his glass. "Plus, this stuff has been ageing down there for years. I reckon it's doing a pretty good job." He sat back and let his head rest against the window. "Anyway. You also need to stop saying what you're actually feeling. People don't want to know that shit."

Raven's mouth fell open. "That is so rude!"

"Exactly," Isaac nodded. "In the city people are rude. If you are not rude back, they will smell weakness and walk all over you. Never say what you mean."

"I'm a full faerie, Isaac, I can't lie."

"I didn't say lie. You just shape the truth into the geometry of what they want to hear. The Folk are great at deception."

"Sure, if there's a good enough reason and you're clever. What you're talking about just sounds like lying."

"*Like* lying, but more civilised." Isaac finished off his drink. "For instance, the truth of what I actually feel is, I think you're beautiful and I'd really like to kiss you right now. But what I'll say is, you're welcome back to the archives anytime. There are very good books, and more excellent wine, at your disposal." He tapped the bottom of her cup, and she was more than glad to pick up his hint and drain it. It was a good way of avoiding a response to what he just said.

"So, are you the faerie that has been trampling all over my

shelving system in the fae literature section?"

"Trampling?" Raven echoed, with mock indignation. "More like 'bringing order to'."

"Hey, I spent a year developing that system."

"A system that makes no sense when applied to fae nomenclature."

"Which is why I went by title rather than author," Isaac argued.

"Making things impossible to find," Raven finished. Isaac grinned.

"There's only one way to settle this," he said. "We pull out the whole shelf, mix them all up, divide the books into two piles, and see who can reorder them the fastest."

"That is, as Nola would say, the most painfully nerdy thing anyone has ever said to me. You're on."

"Wait," Isaac said. "First we each have to drink one more cup to make it interesting." He poured the wine, emptying the bottle.

"Drunk shelving, the scholar's sport," Raven said. They clinked glasses, swallowed the contents, then ran to the shelves.

They only got halfway through putting the books back when Nola and Kofi burst round the corner in a fit of giggles. Nola set an empty bottle on the table, and said, "We may have set off a small alarm somewhere. There's a red flashing light and a beeping noise, it's not very loud but it won't stop."

"And that's our cue," Isaac said, dropping his stack on the shelf unsorted. He hauled himself off the floor, and picked up both wine bottles. They clinked together hollowly. Then he extended a hand and helped Raven up, his fingers cool on hers.

The four of them ducked back through the archives and surfaced above the rusty hatch.

"You were right, Raven," Nola said. "The library *is* fun. Come on, we'll walk you home." She and Kofi walked off holding hands in one direction, and Isaac headed in the other. But not before he surprised Raven by kissing her swiftly on the cheek.

"See you around, little faerie," he said, and disappeared into the night.

The next weekend, Dev arranged a lake trip. They met at Dev's parents' house in the swanky southern suburbs, which was an enormous sandstone structure with a water feature out front. Nola, Kofi, and Dev's latest beau Tom were drinking iced tea in the expansive kitchen with marble bench tops, and Raven was upstairs helping Dev pick out the right sunglasses for the day.

"How many pairs of sunglasses does one boy need?" Raven asked, picking up a cat eye-shaped set with tortoiseshell rims.

Dev tried on another pair, with bright red plastic frames. "Need? Maybe one or two. Want? The number is limitless." He swapped his pair for a classic pair of aviators with an expensive brand printed across the arm. "Do you think Tom would like these better, or these?" He held up the previous red pair.

"Well, I only just met Tom, but I like this pair." She pointed to his face. "How's it going with you two, anyway?"

"Good, fine," Dev said distractedly. "I've decided I don't want a relationship after all. I was never so stressed as I was when I was with Josh."

"Is… that because he pressured you into an arrangement you weren't comfortable with?" Raven held up another pair for Dev to try, with small, circular lenses.

"Probably. But then I figured, skip the drama, sleep around!" He handed the glasses back to Raven, and she swapped them for a pair where you could flip the dark lenses up.

"Weren't you the one who said something about not wanting to have to do one night stands any more?"

Dev discarded that pair too, and put on a neon green pair.

"I was. My new thing is one *week* stands. It doesn't have the sleaziness of a one-night stand, nor the attachment of a month-long fling."

"And how's that working out for you?"

"Delightfully, thanks for asking." Raven said nothing, but Dev sighed. "When you live in a house as large as I do, with very few people in it at any given time, you don't spend any more time alone than you have to."

Raven wasn't sure about that logic, but didn't push him on it. Dev settled on the aviators Raven had originally recommended, and they headed back down the stairs.

The five of them piled into Dev's luxury car, and drove out to the lake district. This was a part of town Raven had never been to before, as it got more and more expensive-looking the closer they got to the water. She had thought that Dev's neighbourhood was posh, but as they drove, the houses got even bigger and more imposing. The gardens, too, seemed to increase in grandeur, with spiral-shaped hedges that were expertly tamed and looked like they needed constant attention. Rose gardens bloomed, an import from the human realm, and the cars in the driveways looked like they had been supplied from Bruce Wayne's own personal collection.

The lake at Cressock was a salt-water affair, with a rickety old jetty where kids jumped off, and overgrown mangroves around its border. There was one run-down aluminium boat that sometimes got taken out, although it was leaky as anything and only fit one or two fae at a time. The shore was pebbly and grey, and there was a tire somewhere at the bottom of the lake where someone had once tried to make a swing but the rope snapped on its way out.

This was not that lake.

Morietta Lake was a pristine pool by a manicured grass lawn. Pastel-striped folding sling-chairs littered the banks, and brightly coloured paddle boats bobbed merrily at a wide dock. Raven somehow felt underdressed. Dev's four guests gazed out in wonder as he unpacked a cheerful, chequered picnic rug, a tray of finger sandwiches, a bottle of champagne, and a carton of peach juice.

"All right, this is the fanciest damn lake day I have ever had," Nola said.

Once, Raven and Arden had gotten into a fight so bad he'd dumped her in the Cressock lake. They had been living in the lake house for about six months, and Arden was dating a harpy with a pet firedrake. It was only the size of house cat, but the harpy always brought it with her and one day, she gave it one of Raven's quilts to sleep on. The next morning, Raven walked out to the couch to find her favourite blanket scorched and ruined. She had gotten angry and kicked the harpy and her firedrake out of the house, resulting in the girl getting extremely offended and dumping Arden on the spot. Arden had then yelled at Raven, who told him she never liked any of the girls he brought round and was glad this one was gone. The whole argument had escalated until, finally, Arden had lifted her up kicking and screaming, carried her out to the jetty, and dropped her off the end. He had instantly regretted it, ran back in the house, and emerged with a thick towel and snacks. They apologised to each other and he fed her peanut butter cookies until she had calmed down enough to come inside.

Kofi was so long his limbs seemed to spill out of the folding chair as he stretched.

"Do all humans have this much money?" Nola asked him. She has gotten up to refresh her drink, and on her way back to her chair Kofi pulled her into his lap.

"No," he replied, "but if it's lakeside champagne you want, I could make it happen."

"Ah, I think I'd get bored quickly," Nola said. "It's only fun because it seems ridiculous. But thanks for the offer." She kissed him on the cheek.

"Well, *I* want lakeside champagne," Tom piped up, holding his glass imperiously out to Dev. Raven rolled her eyes. Of all Dev's recent suitors, Tom was her least favourite.

Raven got up and waded into the lake until the bottom of her wings dipped into the water. She shivered, feeling precious relief from the summer heat. There were no selkies living in this lake, that was for sure.

"Hey, Raven," Dev called, splashing up behind her.

"Hey, Dev."

"So," he said, "Nola tells me you are in need of socialisation."

"I thought I *was* socialising. I'm out, aren't I?"

"I mean, I throw a mean picnic, sure. But this is like, the most basic of basic packages."

"What do you mean, 'packages'?"

"I mean, I think it's time you got the full Dev-fun-times experience. Tomorrow night, we go on a party tour of Repanthe."

"Ugh, Dev that really doesn't sound like my thing."

"Hey, don't knock what you haven't tried!"

Raven rolled her eyes. "I *have* tried it, remember that awful Christmas party? I have no desire for a repeat."

Dev looked offended. "Please. *That* watered down excuse

for a social gathering? These parties will be hand-picked by an event connoisseur."

"And that's you?"

"Yes, of course that's me. My parents are socialites, and I mean *career* socialites. It's in my blood."

Raven sighed. "How many parties exactly are we talking about?"

"I don't know, seven, eight, maybe?"

"*Seven or eight?* Are there even that many parties happening tomorrow night?"

"Of course there are, dear, this is the big smoke."

"It honestly sounds terrible."

"Excellent, I'll tell Nola you're in!"

"What? Dev, I said—"

"I'll ask her to lend you some clothes, too."

"Wait what's wrong with my *clothes?*"

"Okay, good one, Raven, I'll make all the arrangements!"

And with that, Dev headed back to the shore to start his planning.

And so, the very next night, Raven found herself standing on a street corner in uncomfortable shoes and a black dress that had a high neckline but was open at the back almost down to her tailbone. It was Nola's, of course, approved by Dev. Dev himself was in a black bowtie and an outrageously patterned suit jacket. They had decided to leave the first party, and Raven had let herself out before the others had gathered their things. She was sure it was a great party as far as parties went; the thing was, she didn't actually *like* parties. At least not where she didn't know anyone. There were expensive looking canapés in circulation, the cocktails were actually very good, but she couldn't hear a word anyone said and soon gave up trying to have conversations. And then she grew bored very quickly after that.

The second party was quieter, and Raven met beautiful and impressive sounding people who worked in huge corporations and for famous employers. But when they spoke, they just seemed like they must be from a completely different planet to the one Raven was on. Also, they were doing quite a lot of cocaine, which did not appeal since Raven had recently sat by the bedside of a pixie who had had surgery for a nasal perforation due to years of drug use.

By the time they reached the third party, Raven was losing hope fast. Nola and Kofi had each other, and settled easily into different environments. They always found a comfortable couch or a quiet corner to enjoy each other's company. They never excluded Raven, but they did encourage her to meet new people, and Raven didn't want to be a third wheel. Dev seemed to be having a great time; he was travelling solo tonight and had kissed a lot of boys over the course of the night. In between such trysts, he would try to bring Raven samples of food or drink, and introduce her to people he thought she might like. Honestly, he was putting so much effort in that Raven felt touched, and also obliged to keep going.

At the fourth party, however, Raven truly began to run out of steam. She excused herself from a group Dev had pulled her into, and no one really noticed. Raven wandered up the stairs and onto a mezzanine level, looking for a peaceful place to sit for a while. Eventually, she peeked through a set of large wooden doors, slightly ajar. There was a warm light coming from within, and a familiar smell... she opened the door a little further, and saw floor to ceiling bookshelves. Now *this* was her kind of party. Raven slipped through the door and stepped closer to peruse the titles. She trailed her fingers over a row of book spines, and then startled suddenly at the sound of someone clearing their throat.

Raven spun around, and was met with the crooked grin of a pale young man dressed in black.

"*Isaac?*"

"Hello, little faerie," Isaac said. He was perched on the edge of a large mahogany desk, with his arms and ankles crossed, a book tucked into his elbow, and his mouth twitching with bemusement.

"Hey," Raven replied. "What are you doing here?"

Isaac gave her a funny look. "I live here. What are *you* doing here?"

"Oh. Sorry, in that case, I guess I'm snooping."

Isaac laughed. "Well, you're very welcome. This is the best room in the house, so you picked well. I told you I lived in a library."

"Is this your house?"

"It's my grandfather's house," Isaac replied. "I live here with my brother. It's his party."

"How come you're not out there with the rest of them, then?"

Isaac shrugged. "Same reason as you, I'd venture." He stepped towards Raven, and whispered conspiratorially. "I hate people, and also parties."

"Well," Raven whispered back, "lucky for you, I'm fae, so I'm only sort of people."

Isaac laughed louder. "Is that why I like you so much?" He tossed his head towards the door. "Come on, I'll give you the grand tour."

They traipsed back out down the corridor, and Isaac leaned over the railing. He gestured to the mass of moving bodies beneath them.

"The throng," he announced. He moved further down the corridor and opened another door on the right-hand wall.

"The study," he said. Raven poked her head through, taking in a grand, high-backed armchair behind a desk even larger than the one in the library. There was an open journal on it, and a pipe, and a set of half-moon spectacles. The room was smaller than the library, but it also had a floor to ceiling bookshelf with thick, leather-bound books. Isaac stepped back, and Raven followed. He opened the next door.

"The bathroom," he announced. The bathroom was bigger than the study, with huge black and white tiles on the floor and a bathtub that had golden claw feet. It was the most luxurious bathroom Raven had ever seen in her life.

Finally, the corridor ended with small set of stairs. They were shadowy and carpeted, and seemed to lead to a square hatch in the ceiling.

"And up there," Isaac said, "is my room. Do you want to see?"

"You live in the *attic*?" Raven asked.

Isaac chuckled. "I suppose technically I do. Come on up."

He climbed the stairs and pushed the hatch to one side. Raven watched his long legs disappear through the hole in the ceiling, until Isaac called for her to follow. She stepped up tentatively, expecting the smell of dust and mildew. What she saw when her head popped through to the next level, was the complete opposite.

Isaac's room was open and spacious. The floorboards were highly polished, and in the centre of the room was a thick, cream-coloured rug. His large bed was pushed up against the wall in the far corner, with dark sheets and plush-looking cushions, and there was a desk against another that was strewn with books and pens and loose sheafs of paper. In the corner, there was a telescope with a small stool. But, most incredibly, the sloped ceiling was entirely made of glass.

"This is amazing," Raven said, staring in wonder. Isaac took her hand and helped her up onto the floor level.

"Thanks."

The night sky, littered with stars that Raven could not usually see in the middle of the city, stretched out over Isaac's bedroom and lit the space surprisingly brightly. The panels of glass were surrounded by brass frames, and they were crystal clear.

"Yeah, it's hard not to stare. Come on, lie down, it'll strain your neck less."

Isaac pulled her onto his bed and lay on his back next to her.

"How do you keep it clean?" Raven wondered.

"You know, you're the first one who's ever asked me that," Isaac said, amused. "One of the panels opens up, so you can climb out and clean the outside. And the inside I can reach from the floor. It's a bit of work, but I don't have to do it that often, and it's totally worth it."

Raven didn't doubt it. The slow-moving clouds and the softly winking stars made her feel completely at peace, and she felt she could drift off to sleep if she closed her eyes.

"Why would you ever leave here?" she wondered aloud.

Isaac snickered. "To be perfectly honest, I rarely do. I'm pretty much either at home or in the archives. My brother thinks I'm the most boring and useless thing in the Realm."

"Ah, yes, my friends have also been trying to teach me about this 'leaving the house' and 'socialising' business."

"Well, I for one think that they're the mad ones," Isaac said. "It's healthy to enjoy your own company. If people can't be alone with their own thoughts, they need to go to therapy."

Raven laughed. "We all need therapy, I think."

Isaac gestured above them. "This is my therapy."

"You're lucky," Raven said. For a moment, they were quiet.

"Of course," Isaac said, "for a while, *therapy* was my therapy. I went for a year after my parents died, I'm not actually shitting on therapy."

Raven turned to face him. "Oh, I'm really sorry."

Isaac waved her off, but turned to face her, too. "It was a long time ago. And anyway, now I get to live in this cool place."

"Does your brother have a room like this?"

"Nope. We both had rooms on the ground floor, and then one day I found this place and immediately moved all my stuff up here. He's not really the exploring type, so he's happy enough down there. Besides, he goes out and is actually barely home these days."

"What does he do?"

"Uh, finance, corporate something. I don't really know to be honest. He's five years older than me and my polar opposite."

"Do you guys get along?"

"We get along well enough. My dad's gone and granddad's pretty old, so sometimes I think Charlie feels he has to be the big man, or something. Or, at least, he did until I was old enough to take care of myself, and then I didn't really need him any more. So now he's out living his own life. What about you, live with anyone?"

"No, it's just me."

"Ah, lucky you. I would like to live with just you, too." Isaac grinned.

"But if you lived with just me, then I wouldn't be able to live with just me, so it wouldn't really work out."

"No, but then you could live with me, and I'm great

company!"

"Sometimes I miss company," Raven admitted.

"Well, then, sometimes you can come hang out with me."

Raven smiled. "I do always seem to find you in the most fascinating places."

"Well," Isaac turned thoughtful. "To be honest, it's not great up here in the summer because it becomes a little greenhouse during the day. But the archives are always cool, and I'm usually in there until it gets dark and then I come back here. Luckily, summer's just about done. And you are welcome any time to either."

"Thanks," Raven said, hoping she was reading the sincerity in his eyes correctly.

"Just you, though," he said with a wink. "This is not a group invite."

Raven laughed. "I'd feel special if I wasn't pretty sure you're flirting with me."

"Oh, this is my most outrageous flirting, and I actually feel a bit insecure that you can barely tell."

Raven laughed again. "Okay, well, on that note I might have to go find my friends. They'll be migrating soon and will come looking for me."

"Migrating where?"

Raven made a face. "Dev is taking us on a party tour of the city."

"That sounds terrible."

"Honesty, it is. But, also, they are trying really hard to help me find friends and build a life here, and so on, so I want to at least seem like I'm trying. Do you want to come with us?"

Isaac shook his head. "Not if you paid me. But would it help if you could text me live updates about how ridiculous rich people are?"

"You know what, it probably would. But aren't you supposed to be hosting your own party?"

"You found me hiding out in the library, remember? It'd be mutually entertaining. Give me your number." He grinned. "See how smooth I was there?"

Raven rolled her eyes, but took his phone. "You know it's less smooth when you point it out, right?"

"In an endearing way, though," said Isaac.

"Uh huh." Raven handed his phone back. He rang her number so she could save his contact, then walked her back down to the party.

The rest of the night went by much faster. Raven, in a better mood than she had been when they started out, managed to actually enjoy a few conversations. And when she wasn't interested, she texted Isaac.

This house is absurd. No one needs this many giant vases. There isn't even anything inside them.

Isaac wrote back immediately.

If you think that's bad, count the ornamental eggs.

Eggs?

I'm not kidding, have a look.

Raven did, and found eight jewel-encrusted ovaline pieces before they moved onto the next house.

The next morning, Raven was woken by her phone buzzing loudly on the table next to her head. She groaned and tried to ignore it, pulling her pillow over her head until it stopped ringing. But then it started again, loudly and insistently. Raven rolled over and dragged to her ear. The number was private.

"Hello?" she mumbled.

"Lightfoot! Finally, thank the gods. I only have use of this phone for ten minutes and I wasn't sure if you were going to pick up."

Raven sat bolt upright. "Arden?"

His gruff laugh made its way down the phone line. "Sure is, kid," he said. Raven grinned, and then glanced at the phone screen. It was six-thirty a.m.

"You can only call from six-thirty to six-forty in the morning? What kind of prison sentence are you serving over there?"

Arden laughed again. The husky growl of it made Raven's chest ache.

"This is a late start for us, actually. We're usually onsite by six. But since we haven't had telecommunications for months, they're giving us all a turn on this beat up old phone."

"Well, I'm glad to hear from you. How have you been, what's it like over there?" Raven hugged her knees and tried to slow her heart down.

"Why don't you come and find out for yourself?"

"What?"

Raven could hear the grin in his voice. "You, Raven Lightfoot, are cordially invited to the West Bay Housing Project. I've gotten permission from the manager, and we're just about stable enough now that it's not putting out fires every second of every day. So, if you'd like to spend a night out here on the project, I've got a little cabin house thing and you can come stay with me!"

"That… that sounds amazing. Uh, when, where, how?"

"Don't worry, I'll arrange everything and send you the details in the mail. You've got a uni break coming up in about three weeks, right? You could take a weekend off?"

"Yeah, how did you know?"

"Awesome. Keep an eye on the post. Raven, I've gotta call my mum as well in this ten minutes, so I'm going to go now, but we'll have a proper catch up when you get here."

Raven's head spun. She hadn't heard from Arden in over six months.

"Um, okay. Good to talk to you, sort of," she fumbled.

"I know, I'm sorry, hun, but we'll have heaps of time when you get here. I can't wait to see you, and I miss you."

"I miss you too," she said.

Then, all too soon, Arden was gone again.

Raven lay back, stared at the ceiling, and knew there was no getting back to sleep. In a few short weeks, she was going to see Arden.

Six

West Bay

ONE WEEK after Arden's call, an envelope arrived from West Bay. It contained a return train ticket, three photographs, and a short letter in familiar, scratchy handwriting. The thought that if mail arrived within the week then Arden could have been writing this whole time did occur to Raven, but she pushed it back. After all, he had arranged and paid for her trip out.

She put the photos to one side without looking too closely at them (the top one had Arden's face screwed up in a silly pose), and read the letter.

Dear Raven,

I'm so excited for you to get here, I really think you're going to love it. I believe in the project very much, and the only thing that could make it better is if you were here too! So, I figured I would make that happen.

In this envelope you will find your train ticket. I'll pick you up from the station when you get here. I also put some pictures in, there's one of the project before we started so you can tell how much it's changed. There's one of Kita, who cannot wait to meet you. And there's one of my ugly mug in case you forgot what I look like.

See you real soon, kid.

Arden

Kita? Raven scooped up the photographs and flipped through them. Arden looked like Arden, maybe just scruffier around the jaw. The photo of West Bay was mostly a stretch of empty, dry earth, and Raven dropped it to the side. The last photo was Arden with his arms around a girl – a woman, nearly as tall as he was, and with long, auburn hair. She had narrow, hooded eyes and full lips. Behind her, against Arden's shoulder, Raven could just make out the tip of a forked, dark red tail. Was this Arden's girlfriend?

Raven's hands dropped into her lap. She hadn't considered that Arden might have a girlfriend. Suddenly, she was very glad that Arden had told her beforehand, so she could process the information and figure out how she felt about this. Then, she wondered whether Arden had known this would be the case and had given her a warning on purpose.

Raven took a deep breath. She supposed she shouldn't be surprised that Arden had a girlfriend. He was a wonderful person and deserved love, certainly more love than she had ever offered him. So, she stuffed everything back in the envelope and shoved down hard on any feelings she might have about 'Kita'. She felt like she might have a jealousy living in her, but was determined that that was a small and unwelcome guest, and not her herself.

Over the next couple of weeks, Raven busied herself and tried not to think about the trip at all. Whenever she started getting excited about it, she felt nervous about seeing Arden, and then sick about meeting Kita. Easier then, to focus on other things.

Isaac, it turned out, was a fairly effective distraction. One

Wednesday night, Raven was working on an assignment in the library when she got a text from the half-fae.

What are you doing right now? It read.

Studying, she wrote back. *Why?*

I'm at the harbour, Isaac replied. *Come find me.*

Go away, I'm studying.

You're always studying. Come play with me.

Raven shook her head at herself, even as she considered the offer. She did need a break, but the harbour did not have particularly good memories for her. Isaac texted again.

The archives are not the only place I keep secrets.

Raven bit her lip. It would be good to have better connotations with the harbour. She sighed and started packing up her things.

20 minutes, she sent back.

Since the university was in the very centre of the city, it was an easy walk out to the inland harbour on the west side. Raven followed the main road and soon, the sharp tang of rusting metal was faintly burning her nostrils. But Isaac was nowhere to be seen. Raven picked up her phone and called him.

"Hello, little faerie," came the bemused voice.

"Hello, Isaac, I'm here like you asked. Where are you?"

"Can't you see me?" he said, a teasing smile in his voice.

"No…" Raven replied.

"I can see you," he said. "Look a little harder."

Raven squinted out into the night, straining for any signs of movement. And then, closer than she expected, she caught sight of his pale face by a set of railings. Isaac grinned, and Raven put her phone away.

"Welcome," he said, kissing her on the cheek when she reached him. Isaac was leaning against a heavy chain, which stretched out either side of him. He was wearing his customary black, and had a stub of pencil stuck through one of his ears in lieu of the silver circle he had had before. Behind him, there was a drop to the water. It sighed and splashed beneath them.

"So, what's the secret this time?" Raven asked.

"Surprisingly similar to the secret last time," Isaac said. Then he turned and ducked under the chain, and jumped down off the edge.

Raven hurried to the railing and looked over. Isaac wasn't in the water, but standing on the roof of a small boat.

"Coming?" he said. Raven peered out, struggling to make out the shape and size of the roof in the dark. Isaac held out his arms. Raven took a deep breath, then slipped under the chain and jumped towards him, wings flaring slightly to balance herself.

"Wow you really don't weigh anything," Isaac said as he caught her around the waist and lowered her down.

"Gotta have low bone density to get off the ground," Raven said, gesturing to her wings. "Whose boat is this?"

Isaac jumped off the roof and onto the deck, then turned to help Raven down.

"I don't think it's anyone's any more," Isaac replied. "The hull's all smashed in and it's been here as long as I can remember. I've been coming here since we moved to Repanthe, and I've never seen anyone else."

He led Raven into the cabin of the boat, a small space with a squashy bench and—

"You really do live in libraries," Raven said, gazing in wonder around herself.

"Started bringing them down here and my grandfather's never even noticed," Isaac said. The walls, small as they were, were lined with books. Isaac leaned down and opened up a cabinet under the bench. He emerged with two glass bottles.

"The cider he does notice, but I always tell him it's my brother who steals them."

Raven laughed, and took one from him.

At that moment, there was a hollow knock on the roof.

"One second," Isaac said, and ducked out. He returned, and brought someone with him.

"Oh, hey, Kofi," Raven said in surprise.

"Hey, Ray," Kofi greeted her. He had to hunch to get into the room, and when he sat down his legs filled most of the space.

"Where's Nola tonight?" Raven asked.

"Night shift," Kofi responded.

"He gets lonely when she works nights, and I have to babysit him," Isaac said, rolling his eyes. Kofi shook his head.

"That's not true," he argued. "I'm the sitter here." He turned to Raven. "Every time he comes out to the boat, he gets drunk, and I have to make sure he doesn't drown."

"Excuse me, don't make me sound like an alcoholic in front of Raven," Isaac said. Kofi just looked pointedly at the bottle in Isaac's hand.

"Yes, well," Isaac sniffed. "Do you want one or not?"

Kofi laughed his deep laugh, and took a bottle. He clinked it against Raven's and then took a swallow.

"So, what do you guys normally do down here?" Raven asked. In response, Kofi reached into his pocket, and pulled out a battered-looking pack of cards.

"Raven, do you play poker?"

And then suddenly it was the Friday before her trip to West Bay. Raven handed in two papers, attended three meetings at the hospital, looked up the weather on the west coast, and packed accordingly. She texted Isaac back, but didn't respond to his jibes about West Bay being a wasteland. And then, she was on the long train ride to Arden.

Unlike the journey east back to Cressock, the landscape in this direction did not get more colourful. Rather, it morphed from greyscale to sepia, as the environment got drier and the concrete gave way to wheat and straw. Raven slept away most of the trip, and arrived in West Bay as the late summer sun was setting. Her heart thumped in her mouth as she got off the train, and stopped altogether at the sight of the wolfkin on the platform.

"Welcome to paradise!" Arden yelled when he saw her, throwing his arms open. Raven laughed and ran for him, and was scooped up off the ground in a bear hug. The feel of him, here in real life, here with his arms around her and his neck under her nose, was enough to knock the breath out of her.

"Why, thank you!" she said, once he'd put her down again. She took a step back and looked at him though one eye.

"Did you somehow get *bigger*?" she asked.

Arden flexed a bicep. "I may have. All this lifting shit. We're throwing up a house every two weeks at the moment." Indeed, he looked positively squashed into his clothes at the moment.

"You can build a house in two *weeks*?" Raven squeaked.

"Well, the building team is in and out in a fortnight, working ten- or twelve-hour days, then the painting and finishings and stuff are done by the next team. So, we don't technically finish a liveable house in that time."

"That is insanity. That is impossible."

"They're small houses," Arden responded humbly, but pride ruffled over his familiar features. She couldn't help but think of him as a boy with that look when he was first learning to build things with his uncle.

They got in the car, and Raven furtively breathed in the homey scent. Pine, and earth, and wood. She looked over at Arden, and grinned. A warm, happy feeling filled up her chest.

After driving for about a half hour, Arden pulled up outside a little wooden cabin.

"This one's mine," he said. "Bring your stuff in and then I'll show you around the project."

Inside, the house was cosy and sweet. There was a very small kitchen off to one side, and a sofa in the centre. A large window threw long rays of what was left of the sun into the room, giving it a gentle, warm glow. Raven could see three doors off the central room.

Arden led her into the one on the south side of the house. He put her duffel bag down on the bed.

"This one is yours," he said. "Me and Kita are on the other side there."

"Kita lives here too?" asked Raven. The happy feeling evaporated. In the excitement of seeing Arden at the station, she had clean forgotten about his *girlfriend*.

"Yeah, originally it's two to a hut and I was living with this guy James. But then after Kita and I got together, we swapped so Kita could be in here and James is in her old house. That's why we have a spare room now."

"Oh," was all Raven said. The jealous creature shuffled uncomfortably in her chest.

Arden led them back out.

"Bathroom is over here," he said, opening a door on the opposite wall, next to his and Kita's bedroom. "And that's it! Only a tiny place, but you are welcome to anything in it."

Raven smiled. "Pretty sure it's got more rooms than my place in Repanthe, so I'll fit right in."

Arden chuckled. "That's very true, I forgot." He yawned then, and stretched his arms above his head. He was wearing a white t-shirt with 'West Bay Project' printed on the front in bold black lettering, and as he stretched it lifted so his abs were showing, much more pronounced than she remembered. The shirt was working hard to hold itself together over the expanse of his shoulders, but was loose where he slimmed down at the hips. Raven looked away. She remembered how that stomach felt pressed against hers.

"So, are you hungry?" Arden asked. "If you are, I can throw something together. But if you can wait, I'll show you around and we can pick up Kita and get dinner together. I'm pretty excited for you to meet her." Arden beamed at the thought, and the creature dug its claws in painfully.

"I can wait," she said.

Arden walked her around the workers' quarters for a while, introducing her to Folk as they ran into them. Then he led her through the edge of the jungle where it bordered the block of huts. He pointed out small flowers and succulent-like shrubbery, that was so alien from the Cressock forests.

After a couple of hours, they got back in the car and Arden drove her around the project. First, he took her through a small neighbourhood, where they were building houses. One row had been completed, and another row of marked plots sat ready. A couple of structures were half completed, and teams of fae swarmed around the frames.

"Are you supposed to be working still?" Raven asked.

"Nah," replied Arden. "We all get two days off a week. It's just we don't get the same two days so things are always moving forward."

As they drove closer, Raven noticed all the Folk working on

the house had one particular thing in common.

"Woah Arden, you're like the runt of the litter here, are you kidding me?"

They parked the car and Arden laughed. "Yeah, that's how we get them built so quickly. The recruitment process was pretty tough. You had to have a few years of experience. And then when we got here, they divided us on like body type. All the big ones got put to lifting and building, so our whole team is fucking satyrs and centaurs and shit. Then fae who have wings do a lot of fixtures and wiring and stuff. You're allowed to swap if you want but mostly Folk are happy enough with that arrangement and it's just really convenient." Arden laughed. "One time, someone suggested that this dwarf girl Orly help with the painting and she threw a brick at their head."

"Wow, you got centaurs on the project?"

Arden now led her down for a closer look. Fae waved to him, and a few called out, teasing him for slacking off today.

"Yeah, fae have come from all over. Kita's a kitsune, and you know they don't usually come down from the northern regions."

Raven wondered if she was supposed to ask about Kita, but couldn't quite bring herself to do it. Instead, she asked, "So what makes this project so attractive?"

"Well," Arden replied, "it's not just building houses, and it's not just in West Bay. The programme travels around to different remote towns. And we build whatever the community asks for, in this case it was houses but they've done anything from schools to toilet blocks. But the most interesting part is the conservation work."

Soon they left the lot and got back in the car. They were now turning into a trail leading into the thick of the jungle. There was just enough room for Arden's car on the path, but he handled it with ease, continuing to speak as they bumped over the unsealed road.

"During the Realm War, a lot of the environment was destroyed," Arden explained. "So we go through towns that need infrastructure but were also ravaged in the war and need some TLC. West Bay used to have a huge rainforest that led across to the west coast, hence the name. But the forest really got pushed back and the land dried out due to over-farming by the human colonies. And then when the land stopped producing food, the humans left it.

"Now West Bay has a tiny population of Indigenous fae, mostly tree sprites. We have an environmental team who work closely with them, and honestly I don't know enough about that to tell you anything useful, but they do great work. Kita can show you around there later, if you like."

Raven felt torn between feeling interested in the project, and a complete lack of desire to spend extra time with Kita.

They drove slowly and carefully down the path as it got even narrower. Raven sat and stared out the window. There were fae tending plants, taking samples, and a few perched in branches and conversing with the sprites. The forest was a far cry from the thirsty landscape Raven had observed coming out this way, and she wondered how they had found so much life in the dusty earth.

Her reverie was broken by a tap on the window, and she looked to see Arden winding down the window for a beautiful girl in a tight t-shirt that matched his own. The fox girl from the photo.

"Hey, gorgeous," Arden said.

Kita leaned down and folded her arms on the bottom of the window frame. She ducked her head into the car to kiss Arden briefly on the lips, and her russet ears brushed the ceiling.

"Hey, yourself," she said. "Are you come to whisk me away?"

Kita had a soft, husky voice, and a northern accent.

"I am," Arden said. "Are you almost done for the day?"

"Not really, but they can survive an afternoon without me, I think."

Kita walked around to the back door and got into the car. She leaned forward between the two front seats and smiled at Raven.

"I'm Kita," she said.

"Raven." She forced a smile.

Kita might have been Raven's complete antithesis. Where Raven was petite and twiggy, Kita was twice her height and had curves that made her standard issue t-shirt and shorts look incredible, even in work boots and with dirt under her fingernails. She and Arden could be poster children for the project.

Kita had dark, wide-set eyes and high cheekbones typical of northern fae, and she made Raven feel like a pipsqueak. She talked animatedly with Arden and asked Raven questions about Repanthe, and altogether seemed more at ease and comfortable in her own skin while perched on the back seat of Arden's truck than Raven had ever felt anywhere. The jealous creature despaired in Raven's chest. What was the point when *this* was Arden's girlfriend?

"Kita, we're probably about ready to eat, how are you feeling?" Arden asked.

"The same," Kita replied. "I've got fresh fish in the fridge we can have."

"You do? I thought we finished it off," Arden said.

"Yes, but I went fishing this morning, I told you that."

"Oh, I must not have heard you."

Kita rolled her eyes and said conspiratorially to Raven, "Just useless, this one. Can barely feed himself without me."

Raven gave a weak smile, but didn't like what Kita said about Arden. He had always been the more capable one in their friendship.

"Kita's from a fishing tribe," Arden said to her. "Very useful here in a village where the nearest supermarket is an hour drive away, but the water is just on the other side of the forest."

They pulled up at the cabin, and Kita and Arden began pulling things down from cupboards and drawers to prepare dinner. Raven attempted to help, but Kita waved her down. So, she sat on a bar stool and watched the two of them in what looked like a well-worn domestic routine: Arden heated the pan and chopped herbs. Kita filleted and deboned the fish. Then she got to frying while Arden washed and boiled rice. She had never seen Arden like this – so organised and efficient. When they lived in the lake house at Cressock, he mostly ate meat pies and frozen vegetables. By the time dinner was served, Raven found that, actually, she didn't have much appetite.

Of course, Kita and Arden did not have this problem. They both had well-muscled builds and were used to working hard outdoors day in and day out. They inhaled their food, and when Kita commented that Raven wasn't eating much and asked if she felt okay, Arden said, "She's all right, she doesn't eat much. Look how small she is." And suddenly Raven felt like a complete outsider.

Luckily, Arden and Kita went to bed early since they got up at five most mornings. Raven felt it a relief to leave the couple, and ducked into the bathroom to wash off the uncomfortable, heavy feeling that had settled on her like a layer of grime throughout the evening. She turned the water on hot and turned her face up into the steam.

So, okay. The jealousy was not staying down, she had to admit it. Raven closed her eyes and let the water run over her face and into her mouth. She was squandering the small amount of time she had left with Arden, and honestly probably being cold to a perfectly decent kitsune. Raven pressed her fingertips against her eyes, and tried to find a way not to resent Kita. Surely, if she wasn't a terrible person, she could be happy for Arden.

Raven thought about how much she loved Arden and wanted good things for him. She thought about the life he had built out here, how he had supported his family after his dad had died and then moved up and out of their home town to do something world-changing. How he, maybe more than anyone she knew, deserved to be loved, and to be happy. And if he was really happy, then she could be content.

The heavy knot in her stomach began to dissolve, and she turned the water off. Maybe she could do this weekend, after all. Maybe it would be enough to be around Arden for a couple of days and then go back home to the city.

From the bedroom across from hers, Raven heard Kita give a small yelp, and then a giggle. The knot returned.

Raven did not sleep well that night. She got into bed after her shower, but it was much earlier than she was used to sleeping so she sat on her phone for an hour. Then she tossed and turned and slept fitfully, dreaming of foxes chasing her and snapping at her heels. In the early morning, she was awoken by a soft, familiar voice.

"Lightfoot," it said. A gentle hand on her shoulder. "Lightfoot, wake up."

Raven opened her eyes reluctantly. She had never been big on mornings, although the sight of Arden sitting beside her on the

167

bed, his wide yellow eyes shining in the grey light, helped considerably.

"Arden?" she said groggily. "What time is it?"

Arden chuckled, low in his throat. "Early," was all he said. "Come on, let's go for a drive."

"Where's Kita?"

"She's working this morning. It's just you and me."

Raven felt a little guilty, but also glad. She sat up slowly and not fully awake. Next thing she knew, Arden's arms were folding around her and pulling her into his chest. She breathed him in and leaned against him.

"I'm glad you're here," he said into her hair. "Grab a jumper. But you can stay in your pyjamas if you want, we're not going to be around anyone."

Since they were little, Raven always hated getting dressed. For a short time when Raven and Arden were eight years old, Raven's parents gave up the fight and let her wear pyjamas everywhere. This lasted for a week, and Arden had gotten very upset because he wanted to wear pyjamas too, but his mum wouldn't let him. Eventually, Raven had felt sorry for him and started getting dressed so he wouldn't feel so left out.

They climbed into Arden's car, Raven in her plaid flannel pants and oversized knit sweater, and Arden in sweatpants and a t-shirt that hugged his biceps. Raven yawned, and knowing she was slow to fully wake, Arden didn't say anything on the drive.

They drove through a lot of dry, empty land and a stretch of rainforest, before popping out at a vast stretch of beach. Arden came round to open Raven's door, then pulled her out of her seat and onto his back. She smiled into his shoulder. He shut the door behind them and wordlessly began padding down the beach, the muscles in his back moving smoothly beneath her. Then, he picked his way up a steep, rocky trail, and through to a flat shelf, where he finally put her down. Raven stood and stared out at the ocean, wondering if they could see the serpents from here, but Arden took her shoulders and turned her the opposite way.

"Sunrise is this way," he said, and sat down with his legs stretched in front of him and his hands on the ground behind him. Raven settled herself beside him, with her legs crossed.

"Is *that* why you've dragged me out at this unholy hour?" Raven said.

"Worth it, no?"

And she had to confess that it was.

Out in front of them, the forest stretched and yawned beneath the rising sun. The sky was all shades of deep red and roasted orange, and the tops of the trees bounced golden light back up towards them. The air was cool and crisp, and although Raven had never been a morning person, she had to concede there was a certain calm here knowing most living creatures were still asleep. She closed her eyes and breathed in the dawn.

A moment later, Raven opened her eyes and found Arden watching her. His tawny eyes burned in the red light, and she looked away quickly before she could blush.

"So, this is your life," Raven said, making a broad gesture ahead of her.

"I'm a lucky guy," Arden replied.

"You guys are doing some really amazing work out here."

"Ah, it's a tiny project, really."

"You know, I've never seen you care about something so much."

Arden smiled. "Yeah. I guess this is the first really meaningful thing I've done, you know?"

Raven shook her head. "You've looked after your family

most of your life. And you built houses back home, too."

"Sure, but it always felt… kind of small. Like it wouldn't really matter if I did or not. Here, it feels like it matters."

"I don't agree with that, but I get what you mean, I think." Raven hugged her arms across her chest. "And… you and Kita seem to be doing well."

Arden didn't reply, and after a moment Raven looked at him. He had a quizzical look on his face.

"What?" said Raven.

"Do you really want to talk about that?"

"Yes…?" Raven tried. "No, yes really I do. If someone's important to you I want to know about them."

Arden snorted. "You haven't liked a single one of my girlfriends. Ever."

"You haven't liked any of my boyfriends!"

"That's not true, I liked Jasper."

"Jasper cheated on me with Stella Bellamy."

"Jasper's dad had business trips to the Human Realm and brought him back a pet snake. We caught rodents and then fed them to it, it was awesome."

Raven screwed up her nose.

"Okay," she said, after a pause. "Well, I like Kita."

Arden raised an eyebrow. "Do you?" he asked doubtfully.

"Yeah, of course."

"Tell me one thing you like about Kita."

"She's like, the perfect person. She's beautiful and nice and good at everything."

"Okay but what do you actually like about her?"

"She… has a really great backside."

Arden laughed and lay back on the stone. His tail swept out and tickled Raven's elbow. "She does at that," he said.

Raven stared out at the forest and the half-baked daybreak, and tipped her face to the warmth. The colours were starting to mellow as the sun rose. She thought she could see movement among the trees.

"Kita's engaged," Arden said eventually.

"*What?*" Raven whipped her head round to look at Arden, but he hadn't moved and was staring calmly up at the sky.

"Well, almost. Her family is setting up suitors for an arranged marriage. She'll meet them and if they like each other, it's a done deal. She doesn't have to pick anyone, but it's likely she will. She has big plans for her future, she wants to have a family and then take up a leadership position like her mum.

"She's real smart, Kita. She's from a highly respected family in her tribe, and a lot of Folk already expect she'll take over from her mother. And she'll do a great job, too. She's been doing this kind of conservation and justice work since she was in school."

Raven took a moment to digest this information.

"So… where do you come in?" she asked.

Arden shrugged. "She's here for a year before she goes home to get married. She figured she'd have some fun before then, and was up front about it from the start. It's such a small project, a lot of fae pair off. I like her a lot, and it's nice to have the company when you're out in the middle of nowhere. So, it's good for both of us."

"That… sort of sounds like a shitty deal for you though," Raven said.

"I'm happy enough," Arden said. He reached out and touched the bottom of one of Raven's wings.

"But what happens if you fall in love?"

"Well, I guess I could be one of the suitors. Although I'd have to move up north and get married. And I wouldn't be particularly good for her, since I'd be an outsider and she wants someone to help her run the tribe. Plus, I doubt her family would approve of me. All in all, it's not really part of the plan."

"You don't usually *plan* to fall in love," Raven commented.

"Well, that's true," Arden said.

They sat in silence for a time, while the sun kept climbing. She thought she might feel some relief that Kita would eventually leave, but instead she was concerned about Arden. Then, of course, Raven had left him, too.

"You know," Raven said, "I think the last time I was up this early…"

"…Was when you had stayed out all night, fell asleep next to a campfire, and had to leg it back home before your parents woke up."

Raven looked at him sideways.

"Do you have to know everything about me?" she asked.

"I do," he replied, "because unfortunately I was there. For everything."

"Not everything," Raven returned.

"Oh, yes, literally everything. Things I wish I'd never seen, I had a front row seat to."

"Like what?"

"Like the first time you got wasted and puked on my shoes."

"Yeah, okay, well, I bought you new shoes."

"Like the time you spent all night out with that shapeshifter and I had to cover for you, and tell your mum you were with me."

"And I was grateful!"

"Like the time you broke Mrs Flockhart's vase while you were baby sitting and you called me to bring glue so you could repair it before she got home."

"Okay, okay!" Raven threw up her hands. Arden smirked.

172

"You know I know things about you too," she said. Arden snorted.

"You've got nothing on me. You forget I have no shame."

Raven scowled. "When you crashed your mum's car, and I had to come pick you up because the car had to be towed?"

Arden put his nose in the air. "I spent six weeks with Lachlan learning how to repair a car, an immensely valuable set of skills I have used many times since."

"When you fell off the Jamiesons' roof and I drove you to the hospital?"

Arden winked. "Chicks dig scars," he said.

"When you picked up a *rash* from that girl you hooked up with on our road trip to Crownside?"

"Oh, yeah, I forgot about that."

"Pretty embarrassing for you."

Arden gave her a look. "Are you seriously trying to make me feel embarrassed for getting laid?"

Raven rolled her eyes. After a moment, she said, "You know you weren't there for *everything*. Are you sure you were there when I had to sneak back home?"

Arden raised an eyebrow at her. "Sol Cassidy's seventeenth birthday? Oh, I was definitely there."

She laughed. "Oh, yeah. Pretty sure you were the one who made me sneak out in the first place."

Arden wasn't having that. "Ohhh no, you had such a crush on Sol but your parents thought he was bad news and wouldn't let you go. I was going, and you begged me to let you stowaway in my truck."

"Sol Cassidy had a very long, forked tongue; *everyone* had a crush on him."

"Ugh, okay, gross, I do not need to know that."

They fell silent for a while.

Then Raven said, "Making out with him actually kind of *tickled*."

"That's it!"

In the next second Arden had bowled her over and pinned her down, Raven shrieking the whole way. They wrestled around a bit, Arden pretending to be outraged and in truth being careful not to crush her. Until, suddenly, there they were.

Raven flat on her back, the sandy stone gritty against her wings. Arden's body covering hers, his rough hands on her wrists and a stray lock of grey hair brushing her forehead. His torso warm through their clothes. She could feel his heartbeat – or was it just hers?

Months apart and every kiss, every touch they'd shared over Yuletide break came flooding back to her. Raven wasn't sure if her breathing was shallow because she was nervous or because his weight was slightly pressing the air out of her. For a second, his eyes searched hers as the grin faded from his lips.

Arden rolled off her abruptly and sat a few feet away. Raven sat up more slowly, and pulled her knees to her chest.

"Sorry," she said quietly.

"For what?" Arden asked without looking at her. "I'm the one that jumped you."

"For... making things difficult."

"It's okay," Arden said.

Raven sighed. "It's not okay, really. I know I ask a lot from you. I'm always trying to be close to you and keep you at arm's length at the same time."

"It's all right, Raven. I get it."

"But you shouldn't have to," Raven protested. "You must just hate me."

174

"Raven," Arden said, sounding frustrated. "I don't hate you, okay? I obviously don't hate you. I don't really want to talk about this."

"But it's okay if you do," Raven pushed. "You can hate me a bit, and it would be totally fair. I don't want you to be in these crap temporary relationships because of me."

Arden looked at her then, anger suddenly twisting his face.

"Is that what you think I'm doing?" he asked. "You think I'm with Kita because I can't have you? You know, I don't actually think of my relationship as crap, but thank you *so* much for your judgement."

Raven shook her head. "Sorry, Arden, I didn't mean that. You're right, I'm… I'm just projecting because I'm jealous."

"Well, I don't think you get to be jealous!" Arden roared. Raven flinched. "This is what you wanted, Lightfoot. You wanted us not to be together. You wanted to be doing interesting things in the world on your own, but also to know that I would be waiting and available when you were good and ready. You know, I haven't pushed you at all on this, I have actually very fucking cool about this thing where you do or do not want me, but haven't quite made up your mind.

"I wait, and I give you space, and I let you go when you ask, but when I find someone who actually wants to be with me you don't like it."

"I'm sorry," Raven repeated. "I just wanted to…"

"You just wanted to feel less guilty," Arden bit back. "You want me to say I hate you, because your guilt says you should be hated. But you also wanted to hear that I don't hate you. You wanted to make sure that even though you're not around and I'm doing great, that I still love you."

Raven opened her mouth to argue, but no words came. The

words hurt, but deep down, Raven could not disagree.

Arden's chunky work radio chirruped then suddenly, but for a moment they just stared at each other, and no one moved. Then Arden stepped away and spoke into it. When he turned back to her, he was calm.

"Come on," he said. "We need to be getting back."

They made their way back down to the car, and drove in silence. Raven sat miserably, staring out the window, in a puddle of self-loathing and wondered how to make things better. She could see Arden's knuckles clenched on the steering wheel, and although his back was against the seat, the tip of his tail twitched in agitation. She wondered if she should end the misery and beg him to take her back. She wondered if his work on the project and hers in the hospital meant that this was still a good idea despite how bad it felt in moments like this. She wondered if she was actually just too late.

Raven was just about to try speaking to Arden, when they pulled up at the house.

"They want me on site for a few hours," Arden said to her. "You can hang out with Kita for a bit and then I'll come back and drop you back to the train station."

They went inside, and Arden left shortly after pulling some work gear on, leaving Raven alone in the house. She got changed more slowly, and packed her things back into her bag while waiting for Kita.

Ten minutes later, there was a knock on her bedroom door.

"So," Kita said brightly, when Raven had opened it. "Looks like you're with me for the day."

Raven mustered a smile, and followed Kita back into town.

The rest of the afternoon went by in a sort of blur, like she was moving through fog. Kita was working in the lab that day, so Raven was able to sit in with her and not get too in the way. She just had to try keep smiles and interested looks on her face. Kita kept apologising, saying that she knew Arden was supposed to have the day off, but he quite often got pulled in for emergency works. Raven grimaced and waved it off. She didn't want to tell Kita that actually it was probably fortunate that they didn't have to keep having that fight.

Instead, she said, "It must be hard to live on site and always be accessible."

"Yeah," Kita said. "It's tough on Arden."

"Not on you?" Raven asked.

"Well," Kita replied, "I don't really get called in like that. Arden does, because he's the team leader over there."

Raven was surprised. "He is?"

"He didn't tell you?" Kita asked. "It's a relatively new promotion. He's doing really well; Folk listen to him. Something about him… draws Folk to him. Arden's a natural leader."

Raven hid her shock. She hated to think that Kita knew things about Arden that she didn't. And it didn't seem like Arden to take on extra responsibility; he'd never wanted to be in charge of other Folk. Raven had tried to encourage him in the past – he always had such good ideas, if only he would speak up to his uncle, he could have been running that building company straight out of high school. Had Kita managed to inspire him in a way Raven had never done?

Raven shook her head and turned her attention back to the lab. Kita talked her through what she was doing and showed her lots of different samples she had collected in the forest.

"Oh, these ones are edible," Kita said, handing Raven a few different plants. "I only need one specimen but I took a whole bunch because they grow abundantly around the forest floor — and they're delicious!"

Raven picked up a mushroom-looking fungus, and sniffed it. Kita nodded her encouragement, and Raven put it to her lips and chewed slowly.

"Oh man, that *is* good," she said. Kita positively glowed with excitement.

"Isn't it! It's also very high in protein and an extremely sustainable food source."

"How did you get into all this stuff?" she asked the fox girl.

Kita saw down in front of a microscope and turned it as she spoke.

"It's sort of in my blood," she said. "Arden may have mentioned, my mother is the Chief of our village, so my family is very community-oriented. I have an ecology degree, specifically plant ecology, so this project suits me very well."

"Yeah, he said you've been doing this since high school."

Kita nodded without looking up. "Mandatory for me and my siblings. I also have a degree in community development, and a masters in logistics. Pretty much always knew what direction I was headed in."

"Wow," Raven said weakly. But Kita met her eyes and laughed.

"Don't look at me like that," she said. "It's only because I've never had a life; I did one degree straight out of high school and then a double degree after that. I don't have many friends. It's why I usually hook up when I'm on a project. I am, at the centre of it all, very, very boring."

Raven entirely disagreed, but didn't know quite how to argue with Kita's sharp, bright eyes.

Kita was friendly and patient, and explained everything in a

178

way that Raven could understand the complicated work, without being patronising. She was clearly both passionate and competent in her work, and honestly Raven could not find fault with her, despite Arden's jibe about her not liking his girlfriends. In fact, she was downright impressed by the kitsune. And that made it all the worse.

Despite Kita's unwavering positivity, Raven was not enjoying herself. The fight with Arden followed her around like a bad hangover. The lab was too stuffy, and Raven felt clumsy amongst the overcrowded shelves full of glass phials and overhanging vines. Kita's general loveliness just made Raven feel worse about herself, and the jealousy creature paced and snapped inside her. To top it all off, she managed to drop her phone somewhere along the tour and by the time she found it, it had been stomped on by a hoof and was completely unresponsive.

By the time Kita clocked off, Raven was sitting in a corner and just trying not to break anything. Kita handed her a cup of tea, and sat next to her.

"You know," she said, "you mean a great deal to Arden."

Raven sighed. "Yeah. I don't treat him very well, though."

Kita shook her head. "He only speaks well of you."

"Well, that's because he's a much better person than I am."

Kita smiled sympathetically. "He's a good man."

Raven hated herself for asking, but said, "So, you two met on the project?"

Kita nodded. "First day. But it was not, as they say, love at first sight." She grinned. "At first, he was a pain in my ass."

Raven let out a short laugh, in spite of herself.

"It's true," Kita went on. "I've been with the project for two years, and here's this overgrown pup getting under my feet, asking ten thousand questions a day, thinking he knows a better way to organise the schedule. I fantasised about sneaking into his house and cutting off his tail in his sleep." Her lovely eyes twinkled at Raven.

"But, he made me laugh. And he genuinely wanted to learn, and when I started listening to his ideas, I realised not only had he been paying attention but his ideas were really thought through. He had consulted with locals and with management, and only came to me when he was sure he had something worth sharing.

"I've had lovers on projects, but Arden's the first one I've lived with. The first night I moved in, he said your name in his sleep."

Raven looked up, alarmed and embarrassed, but Kita had laughter in her eyes.

"I thought he was complaining about the birds," she said. "I found out later who you were, and I've been excited to meet you ever since."

Raven didn't know what to say.

"Arden is very lucky to have you," she managed. It came out a little hoarse. "I've never been able to get him interested in chasing promotions. Even though he's always been good at what he does."

But Kita shook her head. "That had nothing to do with me," she said. "After a couple of months on the job, he approached management all by himself. Said it was time he became his own person and left a real mark on the world."

"He said that?"

Before Kita could respond, Arden buzzed her phone and let her know he was outside. They drove back to the cabin and Kita made a packed lunch for Raven's train ride, while Arden put her bag in the back seat. He didn't say a word to her on the way home.

The first night I moved in, he said your name in his sleep.

Raven snuck glances at him every so often, but he did not look back.

Eventually, Kita hugged Raven goodbye and Arden drove her to the train station. Several times she tried to say something to him, but the sight of him staring impassively ahead made the words wither and die in her throat. Her heart beat uncomfortably against her ribs.

Finally, Arden parked the car. He cut the engine and leaned his head back against the headrest.

"You know," he said to the windshield, "maybe it's just easier when you're not around."

Raven tried, but couldn't think of anything to say to that.

"I'm sorry for the things I said," he continued. "I was really harsh on you. I agreed to this arrangement and it's not fair of me to turn around and yell at you for us being here."

Now he did look at her, and his molten eyes broke her heart.

"I think this is starting to be a bit unhealthy for both of us, though. I think we should take a break from each other for a while. It'll just... be a bit easier, you know?"

No, she wanted to say. *I just had a break from you and I was miserable. Let's just forget this awful idea and be happy.*

"Maybe you're right," she said finally. "Thanks for the weekend. And I'm sorry."

This time, Raven was determined. She would go with what Arden wanted and stop hurting him so much. She got out of the car and walked to the platform without looking back.

Seven

Twenty-Two

BACK IN the city, it was surprisingly easy to box up her visit to West Bay and hide it in the dusty storage unit of Raven's mind. The rush of the city was a welcome distraction, and truth was, she wasn't ready to think about it. Not with her life in the city going so well and not with Kita in the picture. So, she unpacked her bags as soon as she got home, had a long shower, put a load of laundry on, and soon it was like she had never left.

Well, almost. There was still the matter of her smashed-up phone. When Raven dropped it off at the shop, they told her they'd be able to repair it and probably restore whatever was saved on it, but it'd take a couple of weeks and cost almost as much as a new phone. Raven sighed and agreed resignedly – she disliked the newer models of her phone and had always had a tendency towards sentimentality.

Although she was used to relying on her phone and wasn't keen on being without it, in the end Raven found the loss fairly inconsequential. She was able to video chat with her family and message her friends on her laptop. She had a desk phone at the hospital, and the library communicated via email. It turned out, that just left Isaac to wonder where she had gotten to.

Raven walked in to the library one day for her shift and found the half-fae boy leaning against the counter.

"My goodness," Raven commented. "Am I really seeing you

here, in daylight hours, on the floor of the living?"

"What's a guy to do," Isaac lamented. "You stopped replying to my texts. I thought, it's possible you just don't want to talk to me any more. But then again, I've always been an optimist."

"I'm sorry," Raven said. "I didn't mean to leave you hanging. My phone broke over the weekend and it's still being fixed."

"How will you ever make it up to me?"

"I am in your debt, sir. Consider me your lowly servant until it is repaid."

Isaac's eyes sparked. "Now I like the sound of that," he commented, as he pushed himself off the desk. "I wonder what my first order will be."

"Well, you'll have time to think on it, because for now I am serving my job."

Isaac feigned outrage. "But who will wash my feet? Chew my food? Unsubscribe to my junk emails?"

Raven rolled her eyes. "Did I say servant? I meant magic genie. You can have one wish. *One.*"

"Oh, well, in that case," Isaac said, back to his normal voice. "Go on a date with me Friday night."

Raven paused. She didn't feel ready to go out with anyone. On the other, she wanted very much to prove she wasn't holding onto Arden.

"This weekend I actually have to go house hunting," Raven said, avoiding giving an actual answer.

"You're moving out?" Isaac asked.

"I have to," Raven said. "I love my place, but I'm about to finish up my diploma, and I live in student accommodation."

"That sucks," Isaac said.

"It really does," Raven agreed. "I'm very attached to my

house. Also, I don't know what I'll be able to afford out there."

"How long have you lived there?" he asked.

"Almost a year, if you can believe it." *A year,* she thought suddenly. The thought hadn't occurred to her until Isaac had asked.

"Well, I'll come with you then," Isaac offered.

"Thanks, that's sweet of you," Raven said. "But I've already made plans with Nola."

"Oh. Well, okay, let's go out next weekend then."

Raven opened her mouth to make an excuse, but couldn't find one.

"You owe me a wish, remember?" Isaac grinned.

"Sure," Raven said finally. "Next weekend sounds good."

"So, are you really going to go out with this Isaac guy?" Dev asked. He was lying on Raven's bed with his head and one leg hanging off the side, while Nola helped Raven box up clothing.

"Why not?" Raven said. She was sorting her things into piles – summer clothes and personal books that could be packed away, winter clothes and textbooks that she would need to leave out for her last couple of weeks at uni, and a donation pile of things she didn't want to keep. Nola was assembling cardboard boxes and filling them from the sorted stacks.

"Well… what about Arden?" Dev wasn't helping at all.

"Arden's with Kita," Raven replied. Dev sat up abruptly.

"Who the hell is *Kita*?" he demanded.

"Dev, where have you been?" Nola said, refolding one of Raven's dresses. "I swear, you get so wrapped up in your own chaotic love life you don't listen to what's going on with everyone else."

Dev looked hurt. "My love life isn't chaotic."

Raven looked at him sympathetically. "Yes, honey, it is."

Dev pouted. "Well, okay, catch me up. I'm listening now."

Raven signed. "In summary? Arden's working in West Bay, he lives with his girlfriend Kita. Kita's supposed to get married and run her tribe up north so they probably won't go the distance, but I'm trying to leave him alone and let him be happy. Isaac asked me out and I said yes. The end."

"But... you and Arden are soulmates."

"No, we're just... people." Raven handed Nola a new pile of shirts. "Let's talk about something that's actually important," she said. "Kofi is introducing Nola to his parents tomorrow."

"What?" Dev swivelled around. "You definitely didn't tell me that."

"No," Nola said, "that bit is new. I'm going over to their house for dinner."

"So do they know you're fae?" Dev asked.

"They do not."

"He hasn't told them?"

"We figured if I was there in person, they have to actually meet me before completely rejecting me," Nola said dryly.

"Wow," said Dev, lying back down. "Are you nervous?"

"Terrified. But mostly for Kofi's sake. I don't want him to lose his family because of me."

Raven caught Nola's hand. "If he loses his family over this, it'll be because of them, not because of you." Nola nodded and gave her a wan smile.

"That's what Kofi says." She folded down the tops of a cardboard box and stacked it on the other ones. Raven had never seen her unsure of herself, and it broke her heart a little.

"When's the dinner?" Dev asked.

"Friday night."

"And they're still not talking to Kofi's brother?"

"Nope."

The three of them shared a grim silence for a moment.

Then Nola whizzed the tape roller over a box with a loud ripping sound, and handed the box back to Raven.

"Okay," she said, "that's the last of it, have you got anything else to pack up?"

"No," Raven said, "the rest I'll keep using until I leave." She looked around the room. It was strangely unfamiliar now that her belongings had been removed.

"Okay, well, I'd better get going then," Nola said, standing up. "I'll pick you up on Saturday morning."

"Sounds good. Thanks for helping today. And good luck with Kofi's parents tomorrow."

"Thanks."

After Nola left, Dev ordered food and the two of them ate dinner sitting on the floor.

"So how *is* your chaotic love life, then?" Raven asked him, between slurps of noodles.

"Honestly, not as chaotic any more," Dev said with his mouth full.

"Really?"

"Yeah, I broke up with Chris two weeks ago and haven't seen anyone since."

"Who is… never mind. How come you don't have a new one yet?"

"Because I don't want one."

Raven stared. "Who even are you right now?" she asked.

Dev put his takeout box down. "It turns out," he said, "that after all these people, the best company I've had is my own."

Raven blinked at him. "And you're happy being single?"

"I didn't think I would be," Dev said. "But I deleted the app one day out of frustration, just like full rage-quit the thing, and the anxiety finally stopped. I can hear myself *think* for once. I might get back on eventually, but…" he paused, and shrugged. "Not only am I tall, dark and handsome, I'm also funny and smart and cute. I'm everything I'm looking for." He winked at her, and Raven laughed.

"Still, I don't think you should give up on love. There's someone amazing for you, I am one thousand per cent sure."

"I'm not giving up on love, just dating apps maybe? Also, my therapist says I need to learn to sit with myself and not fill the void with sex."

"Well, I really can't argue with that," she said. She nudged him with her shoulder. "I'm happy you're happy."

Dev grinned. "I'm happy I'm happy too."

The next day at work, Raven ran into a childhood friend. She received a referral like any other day and took one of the gargantuan glass elevators to the fifth floor, then padded across the muted carpet looking for the maternity ward and bed number she had written on her hand.

"*Elodie?*" Raven said in surprise.

"Raven!" squealed the hare-eared fae. Elodie was sitting up in bed, her belly enormous and tucked under a hospital blanket. She looked tired, and maybe a little gaunt in the face, but her smile lit up her eyes. She stretched out her arms towards Raven and wriggled her fingers until Raven was in her embrace.

"Elodie, you're a planet!"

Elodie giggled. "I know! I was due last week, but my babies are just too comfortable in there."

"Babies *plural*?"

"Yep," Elodie said happily, her feet waving under the blanket. She held Raven's hand in one hand, and smoothed the other over her belly. "We're having twins."

"That's amazing! I know you guys always wanted a big family."

"Oh, yes, I think we'll have seven or eight."

Raven laughed, and sat down on the chair beside Elodie. "I take it the pregnancy has been all right then, if that's still the plan."

Elodie frowned. "Not exactly. We've had a few complications but... I'm okay. Marlowe's the one freaking out."

"Marlowe's the one not looking at this through a fog of pregnancy hormones," came a voice behind them. Raven turned, and saw Elodie's partner standing with two coffee cups and what looked like the weight of the world on his shoulders.

"Hey, Marlowe," Raven said.

"Hey, Raven." Marlowe's elven features, usually lovely and sparkling, were drawn and grey. He had heavy bags under his eyes, and his hair was a mess.

He sat down on the edge of the bed and kissed Elodie on the forehead. She looked up at him like he was the sun itself, and cupped her hands around the coffee she was handed.

"Decaf," she winked at Raven.

"So, what are you guys doing all the way out here?" Raven asked them, suddenly worried at the state of Marlowe.

Elodie shot a look at him, then said, gently, "Our doctor back home was getting worried, and wanted us to see a specialist. There aren't any out near Cressock, so we had to come here."

"The drive was awful for Elodie," Marlowe reported, with tortured eyes. "Six hours of bumpy roads, pot holes... she's been so sick as is, and she was in pain the whole drive."

"I'm fine," Elodie said quietly.

"Well, Elodie won't tell you," Marlowe said to Raven. "Poor thing hasn't complained one bit the whole time, didn't say a word on the drive. She already loves those babies so much." Elodie stroked his cheek, and Marlowe leaned into her touch.

"You guys that sounds awful," Raven said. "I'm so sorry it's been a tough pregnancy." She rubbed a hand over Elodie's closest foot.

"It's honestly fine," Elodie said. "We've made it all the way through full term, so I think that means they're safe."

"It's not fine," Marlowe ground out. "Elodie has been in a lot of pain, she gets these awful headaches and can't get out of bed most days. Have you seen the bruises on her stomach?"

Elodie grimaced. "Hare feet," she said. "They're just real good kickers."

"She's on a bunch of different medications. The doctor was leaning towards inducing, but Elodie wouldn't do it and now here we are a week late. Her blood pressure is up, the pain isn't going away, and we've been here since yesterday and no one has seen her."

"You know," Raven said, "I might bring in another fae worker, I don't think I'm supposed to work with you since I know you."

Elodie grabbed at her hand. "Raven, don't leave," she said. "I... I would rather have a friend here than a fae worker."

"You can have both," Raven said.

But when she called down, there was no one else available to attend. One fae worker was off sick, and the other had his hands full. When Raven got back to Elodie's bedside, her eyes widened to see the state of Elodie. She was sitting upright and leaning forward while Marlowe gripped her hand and elbow.

Elodie had paled and sweat glistened on her forehead, her teeth clamping down on her lip and her eyes bright with pain.

"Raven, please," Marlowe begged. "Please get someone to see us, she's not doing well."

Raven hurried off to the nursing station.

"Excuse me?" she said. The nearest nurse looked up from the computer.

"Yes?" he said, with a bored expression. Human.

"Uh, bed five, Elodie Twofinger, is in a lot of pain. Could you go have a look at her please? They say that no one has seen them yet."

The nurse frowned back to the computer.

"Twofinger..." he muttered. "Oh right, the fae woman. Yes, the doctor is very busy."

"Okay, do you think she could have something for the pain while she waits?"

The nurse shook his head. "We don't give pain meds to fae patients."

Raven blanched. "What?"

"Yeah, fae creatures have a higher pain tolerance and don't really need them."

"That... is ridiculous. Elodie is suffering, she looks terrible."

The nurse shrugged. "A lot of them are really good at putting it on, drug-seeking, you know."

"Elodie is not *putting it on*," Raven said furiously. "She's been sick her whole pregnancy, they're here to get specialist help and you need to take her seriously."

"She's probably lying, dear."

"She's *fae* she *can't* lie."

"Yes, well," the nurse replied in a tight, clipped voice. "As I said, the doctor is very busy."

190

"Her blood pressure is up," Raven tried again. "Isn't that bad when you're pregnant?"

"Fae have naturally higher blood pressure, I wouldn't worry about it," the nurse said.

"No. We. *Don't.*" Raven pushed out. "Not only is everything you're saying extremely discriminatory, it's also just factually incorrect. Elodie is in *pain*. I have known that girl since we were five and she has never taken illicit drugs in her life, she's not an addict, she doesn't have a different scale for blood pressure, and someone needs to bloody see her!"

The nurse just blinked at her. "You know her?" he said. "I don't think you can be working with her in a professional capacity if you have a personal connection."

Raven resisted the urge to slap him across the face, and stalked over to the phone on the desk. She punched in the number for the other fae worker.

"Aubrey?" she said through gritted teeth. "I need you to come to the maternity ward."

"Sorry, sport," the old dwarf said down the line. "I'm still over in Heart Lung with this nixie family."

"Swap," Raven snarled.

At the end of the day, Raven walked home in the dying light, exhausted. Aubrey had come up once Raven told him what was happening, and he had gone over the nurse and straight to the senior doctor. Once you got Aubrey started, there was no shutting him up. He hounded the doctor and lectured about discrimination until the doctor finally threw his hands up and went to see Elodie. Aubrey winked at Raven.

In the end, they did have to induce Elodie. The doctor grumbled at first, but then her tests came back and she was taken immediately to the induction clinic. Raven saw her go, and promised to come back on Monday morning to see them all.

On her way home, she felt relieved that Elodie had gotten the treatment she needed, but was very disturbed by what the nurse had said about fae patients. Aubrey had told her to relax over the weekend, then booked a time with her so they could sit and debrief about it properly the next week.

Saturday dawned sunny and bright. Raven poured out two cups of coffee waiting for Nola, and stared down her dissertation. She had four weeks before she had to hand it in, and although she had done a lot of research for it, she hadn't written a word. The episode with Elodie in hospital had her rattled, and it was suddenly very difficult to write academically about a subject that was now very emotionally raw.

Eventually, there was a knock at the door, and Raven closed her laptop gratefully. It would be good to see Nola; if anyone understood about prejudice in the hospital it would be her.

She opened the door, and greeted her friend.

"Morning—oh. Hey, Kofi." She hadn't been expecting Nola's boyfriend, too. Then she noticed how serious they both looked.

"Is… everything okay?"

"Raven?" Nola began. "Do you mind if Kofi comes house hunting, too?"

Raven brought them in and made a third cup of coffee. They all sat in Raven's bare living room, while Nola recounted the previous night's events.

Kofi had brought Nola home to his parents' house for dinner. They took one look at Nola's green face, and a shouting match broke out. Nola and Kofi's hopes that meeting her in person would – for lack of a better word – humanise her, were quickly and thoroughly dashed, thrown forcefully in the garbage along with the roast his father had so diligently prepared.

Nola had tried to stay out of it, not wanting to make the situation worse. But his parents said horrible things about the Folk, and about her, and about Kofi. Eventually, she had snapped and yelled back in defence of all three. Kofi's parents went silent, as if deeply offended that she had dared speak to them. After a moment, his mother had turned to Kofi, and ordered him out of the house. Then she had her husband had retreated into the kitchen without another word, and didn't come back out.

Kofi's bedroom was in the front of the house, so they had spent five minutes in there stuffing some essentials into a backpack. Then they shut the door behind them, and Kofi did not look back. They spent the night in Nola's cramped studio, and Nola had stroked his head until he fell asleep.

"So," Nola sighed. Her eyes were teary, but her mouth smiled. "We are now looking for a slightly bigger place where we both can live." She squeezed Kofi's hand, and he kissed her temple. "And we were wondering if you wanted to live with us. We can find somewhere pretty decent with rent split between three."

Raven was speechless. "I... yes. I would love that. And, Kofi, I'm so sorry."

Kofi smiled at her. "Thank you. But don't be. I love Nola, and my parents need to accept that. They chose to shut us out of their lives, nobody else made them do that. It is ridiculous that they are living on fae land and they still think fae are somehow beneath them. And I still have my brother, so I haven't lost my whole family."

"Will and his husband have been so supportive," Nola said.

"They offered for us to move in with them, but they've got a baby, so we didn't want to take up their space."

"Anyway, now we're looking for a fresh start," said Kofi.

"I'm glad you're okay," Raven said. "Can I hug you guys?"

Kofi laughed, and the three of them wrapped themselves in a group hug.

Nola was the first to break away, briskly wiping her eyes.

"Okay!" she said. "Enough seriousness and sadness! Now, I was feeling very guilty last night and couldn't sleep," – here, Kofi snorted disapprovingly and kissed her knuckles – "so I looked up a bunch of places for lease and made a list of the top five."

They piled into Nola's station wagon and set off. Raven had brought snacks for all of them, and chewed on a twist of raspberry liquorice while she flicked through Nola's selection. Nola had done a great job, the five places were all reasonably priced, decent-sized, two-bedroom places, not far from the city centre.

"You guys, this is our first adventure as a house group!" Raven said. She was keen to be sharing again; although she had enjoyed living alone, it did get lonely at times. Being introverted meant that without a built-in social system, she often forgot to see other people for days at a time.

"Well, it might be closely followed by a second," Nola said. "I don't know if we have time to get to all five places today, and also if all of these are no good, I have some back-ups we can see tomorrow."

In the end, though, there was no need. The very first apartment on Nola's list was perfect. It was in a building with lots of other fae residents, and there were big open spaces that made the place look larger than it actually was. The walls were white and the windows were huge, letting in decadent pools of natural light. On the floor, the thick carpeting was soft and springy underfoot. The bedrooms were at opposite ends of the house, the one furthest from the front door opening up onto a small balcony overhung with green, leafy branches. Nola put her hand on the bark and smiled fondly.

"This is a happy tree," she said. Kofi came up behind her and wrapped his arms around her waist.

"What is it telling you, love?"

Nola closed her eyes. The language of trees was unspoken, and not so precise. But she could feel its emotions and memories.

"The tree is not very old. It likes living here, where it can see inside and feel like part of the family."

They went to see the other places, but after being in the first apartment, none of the others seemed appealing any more. One was too dark, the next slightly mouldy. Another was next to a main road and extremely loud, and the last one was nice except that you had to go out the back door to get to the bathroom outside. They breezed through them and left quickly.

Kofi drove them all back to Raven's place, and they chattered excitedly in the car.

"I mean, it's the first one, right? It's got to be."

"For sure," Nola said, turning around in her seat to speak to Raven in the back. "It's a little more expensive than the other places…"

"But it's so much better," Raven finished. "That balcony is perfect for you, Nola."

"Oh," Nola said. "I wasn't going to assume…"

"Of course you'll have that room. You guys are a couple, you need the bigger room. Plus, you're a tree nymph, it's a no brainer. I actually like the other room anyway. It has that great built-in wardrobe with so much space, I'm going to half fill it with books!"

Nola turned back to Kofi. "What do you think, baby?"

Kofi grinned. "I love it."

Nola glowed. "It's close to your brother as well."

"I noticed," Kofi said. "Thank you, for that." He squeezed her hand.

And so, it was settled. They applied for the lease, and a week later they had been accepted. Raven felt slightly better about leaving her beloved townhouse, knowing she was moving in with some of her favourite people. Nola and Kofi would be moving in immediately, and Raven would join them as soon as she was done with the semester.

The next weekend, Raven went out with Isaac. He met her at the library as her shift was ending.

"Still no phone?" he asked. Raven pulled a face.

"I went in this morning, and they said it still wasn't ready. Apparently they don't fix it in-store, they send it away. And they haven't gotten it back yet, even though repairs should be done by now."

She ducked into the bathroom to freshen up before they left. She pulled her hair up into a ponytail and put on lipstick. She took off her stockings and changed her shoes. Finally, she dabbed a little perfume behind her ears. Then she went back out to where Isaac was waiting.

Isaac put his hand over his heart, and sighed. "I am a lucky man," he said. He picked up a large bag and slung it over his shoulder, before taking her hand.

"Where are we going?" Raven asked.

"Not far," Isaac said.

They walked across the university grounds and out onto a large grass field. Dusk was settling in, and the sky was purpling bruises. Once they were in the middle, Isaac stopped. He licked his finger and tested the wind, and then tapped his foot on the ground in a few different places, listening intently.

"Yep," he said, with a frown of concentration on his face. "This is the spot." Then he plonked himself down on the ground and began pulling things out of his backpack: a picnic rug, some wrapped sandwiches, and a bottle of sparkling wine. Raven sat down opposite him.

"We're not about to get run over by a football team or something, are we?"

Isaac shook his head. "Nope, today the field has been booked by the whiskey ball team." Raven raised an eyebrow.

"That's us," he said in a stage-whisper. Raven laughed.

"So, we're playing whiskey ball?"

"Well, it'll be a bit difficult because I made it up. But, yes, let's play."

"Okay, how do you play?"

"I haven't thought up that part yet, give me a second." Isaac put a finger on his chin, and put on an air of being deep in thought. Raven laughed again.

"Okay, first, we have to eat these sandwiches. I made them myself. They are very delicious. You also get points for each accompanying glass of wine."

He handed her a wrapped triangle, and poured their drinks.

"Did you cut the crusts off?" Raven asked, surprised, as she unwrapped her sandwich.

"But of course. Crusts are for peasants." He handed her a glass.

"Oh." Raven made a face. "The wine is not as good as the sandwich."

"No, well, the wine is very cheap. I have not yet inherited

197

anything from my filthy rich grandfather. But the drunker you get, the less unpleasant the taste is." He clinked his glass against hers.

"Are you going to try get me drunk every time you see me?" Raven teased.

"Only when I see you outside of daylight hours."

"So, every time."

"Yeah, pretty much."

Raven rolled her eyes, and ate her sandwich. It really was very good.

As they ate, Isaac kept listing out rules for whiskey ball, as they came to him.

"Rule thirteen," he said with his mouth full.

"Fourteen," Raven giggled.

"What?"

"You're up to fourteen."

"Oh," Isaac said. What was rule thirteen?"

"Rule thirteen was you can't score a goal if your shoes are on."

"Ah yes. Rule fourteen is, if you do score a goal but your mouth is full, that's a negative point. One to the other team."

"Wait, how do you score a goal?"

Isaac closed one eye. "You score a goal by getting the ball over the floozle line."

"And that's the one after the limbo stick but before the fencing circle, yes?"

Isaac nodded. "That's right."

"But rule eight was no balls," Raven pointed out. Isaac looked outraged.

"Why would a game I make exclude balls?"

"I don't know how to respond to that."

"Ha! That's rule four, you have to drink." Isaac tipped the bottle over her glass.

When they had finished eating, Isaac conscientiously balled up the papers from the sandwiches and put them back in his bag.

"Okay for the next part of the game, we star-gaze." He flopped back onto the grass. Raven laid down more slowly.

"Isaac?" she said.

"Mm?"

"There are no stars. We're in the middle of the city."

Isaac sighed. "There are still stars, you just can't see them."

"Right. Well, how do we star-gaze if we can't see stars?"

"Oh, I can see them."

Raven looked at him. "You can?"

"My mother was fae, remember?" Then it clicked.

"Wait, can you see in the dark?" she asked.

"Yep." It suddenly made sense how easily Isaac had moved around the dark harbour, when she could barely see him. "It's why you don't see me in the daytime very often. The sun hurts my eyes, it's too bright." Isaac stared up at the sky, and pointed over to their left. "That's Orion, there." Raven strained to make out the constellation, but saw nothing.

"What kind of fae was your mother?" she asked.

"She was a siren. Had legs in the day and a tail at night. When my parents were alive, we all lived on the coast. She would disappear down into the black water, most nights, and it always scared my father. But I could see her perfectly, so I wasn't afraid."

Raven wanted to ask how they had died, but she felt like it might be rude. Instead, she asked, "And you're able to lie?"

"I am. But I don't do it very often."

"Can your brother see in the dark, too?"

Isaac shook his head. He rolled over onto his side, and looked at Raven.

"My brother takes after my dad. Everyone always said I was like Ma."

"I'm the opposite," Raven said. "My little siblings look like my mother, but I've always—" Isaac interrupted her thought by kissing her.

"You have the blackest eyes," he murmured. "I can see stars in them, too." Then he kissed her again, with fresh bread and cheap wine on his lips.

And no bubbles or fizz appeared at all.

Raven spent the next two weeks staring down her dissertation. Starting was always the hardest part – once she got the first few words down, the rest usually came more easily. After visiting Elodie and her twins in hospital, all three safe and sound, Raven decided to ask Elodie to be a case study in her paper. She explained to her that all the details would be anonymised, and Elodie heartily agreed to it. Marlowe took them all home as soon as they were allowed out, muttering that he would be glad to see the last of this hospital and of Repanthe. But he also brought flowers for Raven as a thank you.

Nola and Kofi settled into the new place, and they even came and picked up some of Raven's boxes so that she could focus on writing. There were a few bits of paperwork to complete for both moving out of the town house, and into the new one, but they languished on the end of Raven's bed while she focused on her essay. The store emailed to say her phone would be ready for pick-up by the end of the week, and that job too went on the back burner.

Isaac smuggled coffee into the library while she studied, but, apart from that, she didn't see much of him over the weeks since their date. One time, he was finishing a work shift and she was still there, hunched over a desk. He persuaded her to take a break, and pulled her up out of her chair.

"You keep staring at those books and you'll give yourself a headache, I should know," he said. He took her hand and dragged her away from the desk.

"Too late," Raven groaned. Isaac chuckled and led her to a grassy patch outside, flicking sunglasses from his head to his nose.

"I prescribe vitamin D, and focusing your eyes on long distances for a while," he said. Raven stretched her legs out and tipped her face to the late afternoon sun.

"Okay, this was a good idea," she admitted. Isaac's hands came up to knead her shoulders.

"Let me guess," he said, "you're also sore from looking down at your laptop all day." Raven just hissed in response as his fingers found a particularly tight knot.

"Yeah, I know," Isaac said. "I've been there."

They sat for a while longer, and Isaac did impressions of the head librarian. Raven laughed and felt the stress leak out of her, and was glad she had been forced on a break.

Until Isaac's face changed, as he watched her laugh. His twinkling eyes got serious, and he leaned in to brush a stray curl from her face. His pale fingers grazed her cheekbone, and she pulled away a little.

"I should get back," Raven said quietly.

"Okay," Isaac said. "Drink this." He handed her a bottle of water, and she thanked him then disappeared back into the library before he could say anything else.

After that, Raven started avoiding him a bit. While she was

very fond of Isaac, she couldn't help thinking about how it had felt to kiss Arden, and how kissing Isaac had not felt like that.

In fact, when she thought about it too long, the guilt rolled like nausea in her stomach. Clearly, a part of her just wanted Arden. But she had said 'no' to him when he wanted her, and now he was with Kita and not speaking to her at all. So, she thought she would be fair to Arden finally, and try to move on. Isaac was witty, and sweet, and there was no earthly reason she couldn't make it work with him. But if her heart wasn't truly in it, was she now just hurting Isaac the same way she had hurt Arden?

No, Raven did not have the brain space to figure this out while she was trying to finish her diploma. Work on your own accomplishments, then figure out your love life: that was the going principle for her city life.

Chicken-shit, said a voice in her head.

Time went by in a blur, and before she knew it, she was sitting opposite Nola on her bed, while Nola leafed through a spiral bound copy of her finished paper.

"*Discharge against medical advice: Outcomes for fae patients in tertiary health settings,*" Nola read. "Big words!"

"Yeah, but is it any good?" Raven asked, anxiously chewing her nails.

"Raven, this looks great."

"Really?"

"For sure. It's very thorough, and the more fae writing about fae experiences, the better."

"Thanks, Nola."

"No need to thank me, it's true."

Raven handed in the paper that afternoon, and Nola threw her a small celebration at the new house. Nola and Kofi had furnished the house beautifully. They had moved Raven's old armchair in, as well as a brown leather sofa, and several large potted plants from Nola's studio. Kofi's brother, Will, had donated some deep blue drapes, and matching cushions. The effect was a warm and welcoming space, where Raven immediately felt at home.

Dev brought a house-warming gift, a fancy espresso machine that was being replaced at his house with an even fancier one.

Isaac arrived with fifteen balloons spelling out 'congratulations', although almost immediately lost several out the balcony, so he rearranged the remaining letters to spell 'contagion', which he said was still relevant to her paper.

Kofi made giant pizzas for dinner, and then Dev produced a guitar and played a surprisingly moving song of his own composition.

"That was amazing, Dev!" Nola told him.

"Thanks," Dev said.

"No really, I had no idea you could do that."

"Okay, well, you don't have sound so shocked," he grumbled. And then, under his breath, "You guys never come to my gigs."

Raven shot a guilty look at Nola, because that was true, and Nola shrugged back as if to say, *to be fair to us the band always sounded like a disaster.*

After that, he and Kofi started up a video game while Nola dozed off on the couch.

"Let's go for a walk," Isaac said quietly in Raven's ear.

Raven and Isaac strolled around her new neighbourhood. It was a bit further out from the city than Raven's old townhouse, and some streets were quite dark, where the heart of Repanthe was lit always. Isaac tucked her arm in his, and she felt safe in the knowledge that Isaac could see where they were going. They found a small park with a fountain, and sat on the edge. Bright copper pennies winked up at them, gleaming in the moonlight. For a while, Isaac said nothing. He stared out in front of them.

"Raven, I have to ask you something," he said eventually.

"Okay?" She waited.

"Do you… do you actually want to be with me?"

Raven blinked in surprise. "I…"

"I mean, I really do think you are amazing," Isaac continued. "And I really hope I'm wrong about this. But it's been two weeks since we kissed in the park, and I've barely seen or heard from you."

"I've… been so busy with my studies," Raven said lamely.

"I know," Isaac said. "But even then. I think you've never been quite as keen for this as I have."

Raven searched for the words. He was right.

"And it's okay," he continued, "if you don't want to be with me. I still really like you and I will still be your friend. If that's what you want." He paused, and looked at her. "Is it? Is that what you want from me?"

Raven exhaled and looked back at him. "Yes," she said. "I'm so sorry. You're right."

"I usually am," Isaac said ruefully.

"I've been so unfair on you, and I am the worst person."

"Only a little," Isaac teased.

"It's just that… I so *wanted* to want you. You're amazing and I think there's something very wrong with me."

"There's nothing wrong with you, little faerie."

"I'm really sorry."

Isaac kissed her the back of her hand swiftly before letting it go.

"Never apologise for wanting what you want," he said. "Or for not wanting what you don't."

It was three days before Raven was due to move out of her beloved townhouse. It was also, incidentally, three days before her twenty-second birthday, which Dev had been obsessing over for the last week. Raven had wanted to go home for her birthday, but Nix had picked up a stomach bug from one of the kids at school, and Cecelia said it wasn't a good idea to come back. Raven was disappointed, but also knew it wouldn't have been the same without Arden anyway. Arden himself hadn't gotten in contact; there were no emails or messages from him on her computer, and so Raven was not in a particularly celebratory mood. Dev, however, having been contentedly single for over a month, needed a project to put his newfound energy towards.

"Raven, you will be the guest of honour so you can't arrive until seven-thirty," Dev said to the group. They were gathered in the living room of the new house, while Dev stood in front of a white board covered in symbols none of them understood.

"Your entrance of course comes from here," he said, tapping a square that Raven assumed was the front door. "Nola, your station is here," he continued, indicating a triangle that might have been a fern, "and Kofi will be here."

"At... the... squiggly circle thing?"

"The ice sculpture!" Dev said exasperatedly.

"There's an *ice sculpture?*"

Dev fixed him with a stern glare. "We talked about this."

"I don't remember..."

"Nola!" Dev barked. "Will you get your man under control?"

"Sorry, Dev, I don't remember that either," Nola admitted. "Where are we going to get an ice sculpture?"

Dev pinched the bridge of his nose and sighed. "My parents. Have an ice sculpture guy. Who will be delivering. At six p.m."

Isaac raised a hand. "I thought the six p.m. delivery was the chocolate fountain."

"The chocolate *what?*"

"HAS ANYONE BEEN LISTENING AT ALL?" Dev bellowed.

"Woah, okay," Raven said, standing up. "Dev, this is lovely, really, but I don't need some massive party. Pretty sure I don't know half the people on the guest list. Honestly, I just want to hang out with you guys. And, actually, yeah, the chocolate fountain sounds pretty great, let's keep that."

"No no no no," Dev said, putting his hands on Raven's arms. "Honey, you are way too small-town! You only turn twenty-two once!"

"Yeah," said Raven, "but with any luck I'll turn twenty-three, then twenty-four, and so on. And for the record, my twenty-first was pretty rad. I don't need another big event."

"You… don't…" Dev spluttered. He opened and closed his mouth several times, soundlessly.

"Raven, I think you broke him," Isaac said.

Dev took a deep breath, then turned to the whiteboard.

"Isaac, you will be stationed here," he said, pointing to a rectangle, and appearing to be ignoring the last five minutes of conversation. Everyone else groaned, and Dev soldiered on.

Two days before the big move, Raven quit her job at the library and took up full time hours at the hospital. The job felt meaningful, the money would be better, and now that Raven was done with her diploma, there wasn't much reason to be in the library all the time. Plus, although she rarely saw him, she knew Isaac was right downstairs. They had been amicable since their talk at the fountain, but Raven thought it best to give him some space. She didn't want to repeat the mistakes she had made with Arden, and make things harder on him that need be.

One day before her birthday, Raven dropped off the bags of things she was donating, and packed the remaining things she still had in her house. It all fit into just one box. She walked around the house and said a silent thank you to the walls, the stairs, the fireplace. It had been a wonderful place to live and to come home to.

On September the fourth, Raven woke in her bare, empty house, and wanted to cry. This was the first time in her life that she had had a birthday without Arden. With their mothers so close, they had always gotten together when they were children. And after Arden's father died, and the Slivers didn't feel much like partying, the Lightfoots made sure to celebrate Arden twice as hard, every year.

Raven walked around the house. It was very quiet. She sat in the middle of the living room, the morning air chilling her bare arms, and took stock of her year in Repanthe. She was a year older, and she had completed her diploma. She had a good job, and felt like she was making a difference in the community with it. She had gorgeous friends who were throwing her an excessively large party tonight. It was everything she had wanted when she moved out of Cressock. So why did she feel miserable today? Did the fact that she couldn't have Arden really cancel everything else out?

Of course not, Raven thought to herself. *They are all things I wanted to achieve. I'll just have to work on not wanting Arden because he doesn't want me and he deserves to be happy.*

But was that true? Memories of Arden looped through Raven's mind, and she had to acknowledge that he had never rejected her. Sure, he had Kita. But he had said that wasn't serious, right? Their only barrier had been Raven, over and over again.

She shook he head to clear it. *But I was being sensible,* she reasoned. *I needed to live my own life. Figure out what I wanted. Have achievements of my own.*

Which surely she had just established that she *had* done this year. Raven's heart began to beat uncomfortably fast. She got up and started pacing to try to dissipate the nervous energy that was building in her chest.

What was she doing? What was the end goal here? When would one be old enough or ready enough or accomplished enough to be allowed to fall in love? And if it had been a year, and she could live on her own and thrive, and even after everything else she still wanted Arden like a heartbeat, was now a good a time as any to let them both off the hook?

Raven stopped in her tracks.

"You're such an idiot," she said out loud. The empty room agreed.

From across the room, her laptop pinged with a notification alert: one new email. Raven crossed to where the computer was charging, and found an email that had been sent the day before.

Dear Ms Lightfoot,

Please be advised that your mobile phone is ready for collection. We apologise for the delay and for any inconvenience this may have caused. We are open from 9 a.m. to 5 p.m., every day except

Sunday. Your reference number is 514-627.

Kind regards,
  The team at Phone World.

Raven glanced up at the little clock on the screen: 8.46 a.m. It would take twenty minutes to walk to the shop. Raven threw on some random clothes from the top of her box, and headed out.

Forty minutes later, she arrived home with a repaired but battery-flat phone. She plugged it in to charge, and thought about what she would say to Arden.

Happy birthday, Sliver. Also, I love you.

Okay, not that. Something heartfelt, and meaningful. Something that would make up for the awful argument they had the last time they saw each other. There was a terrifying thought – did he even still want her any more? Had she left it too late? Had she pushed him away too hard? The months of pointed silence did not bode well. Perhaps Arden didn't want to hear from her. Perhaps he would still be angry.

Then again, the point might be moot. Arden was in West Bay after all, with a famous lack of reception. She might not be able to talk to him at all.

Raven pressed the 'on' button on her phone several times. Still nothing. So, she got on with her morning routine to give herself something to do. She washed her face, brushed her teeth, and pulled her hair into a braid. She put on a nicer top and some mascara. She got half way through a second coat of nail polish when her phone finally buzzed to life.

Raven lunged across her bed and snatched up the phone. A handful of unanswered texts flashed up, from what had now been almost a month of being without a phone. And then – one missed call from Arden.

Raven dialled voicemail, then pressed the phone to her ear with her heart in her mouth.

"*You have one new voicemail,*" came the mechanical voice. "*From, Arden Sliver, on the fifth of August.*" Two days after she left West Bay. And then, her favourite husky voice crackled down the line.

"Raven?" he said. Tears sprang to Raven's eyes. "It's me. I, ah, shit." There was a pause.

"It's Nyetak, you only left a couple days ago. And I've been trying to figure out how to turn back time since then. As soon as you were gone, I regretted it all. It's not easier without you, of course it isn't, that was the dumbest shit I've ever said. I… I broke up with Kita. I think we could make it with other people if we really tried, but honest to gods, I just don't want to. And I'm hoping that across the country, you're finding the same thing." He barked out a laugh. "And then I drove halfway to Linkhaven just to get some reception. My manager's not too happy with me. But I just want you to know that I'm not half-assing things any more. I'm in, Lightfoot. You're it for me, and you know it. I know there's some stuff you gotta do first, and I know you haven't decided yet, so I'll be here. For as long as it takes you to find your way back to me.

"Anyway. That's about all I've got to say. And also, I love you."

There was a rustling, then a beep.

"*End of messages.*"

Raven swiped at her eyes and sniffed. She hit they key for replay, and listened again.

"I'm in, Lightfoot. You're it for me, and you know it. I know there's some stuff you gotta do first, and I know you haven't decided yet, so I'll be here. For as long as it takes you to find your way back to me."

Raven hit redial, and pressed the phone to her ear so hard it hurt. The phone rang and rang. She hung up and dialled again. Still nothing.

"Fuck!" Raven yelled out loud.

"Hey, you've reached Arden's phone, leave me a message."

"Hey, Arden," Raven said, her voice shaky with tears. She sniffed and laughed. "Happy birthday, Sliver. And also, I love you." She went to end the call, then added, "And I'm sorry it's taken me so long."

She hung up and immediately dialled Arden's mother.

"Hey, Annabelle," she said, trying to keep her voice steady and bright.

"Hello sweetheart, happy birthday!" Annabelle sang. "How are you, darling?"

"Thank you! Yeah, I'm good. Hey, is Arden home?"

"No, honey, he's still in West Bay. We wanted him to come back but they aren't letting him go just yet. They're almost done, though, we're expecting him back next weekend."

"Oh, okay, thanks."

"You haven't heard from him?" she asked.

"Uh, yeah I just did. Sort of."

"Okay well you make sure he's being nice to you, and you let me know if he isn't."

Raven laughed. "Arden's always nice to me."

"Well that's almost certainly not true, but you're sweet for saying so."

She laughed again. "Okay, well, I'd better call my parents, too."

"Sure thing, sugar, have a lovely day. Hope to see you home

soon!"

"Thanks, Annabelle. Speak to you later."

They hung up. Raven did not call her parents.

So, Arden was still in West Bay, and not contactable by phone. Okay, but he would be home next weekend and she was definitely due for a trip back anyway; she hadn't been back to Cressock since last Yule. But that would mean waiting a week, and that was just not tolerable. So she'd go to West Bay, and find him.

But the West Bay was a remote area and last time she'd been, they'd had to drive into the village from the train station. Well, she'd just have to figure it out. The train trip was quite long enough to figure out a plan. Although she'd almost certainly miss her own birthday party, and Dev had gone to so much effort...

Raven pushed the thought to the back of her mind. It didn't matter. She'd try to make it back, or she'd explain it to him later. She had to get to Arden. Raven snatched her coat off its hook and shoved her phone, keys and wallet into her pockets. She pushed her feet into her boots without pausing to do up the laces, and headed for the door. She could be at the train station in fifteen if she walked fast.

Raven fumbled with the lock for a second, then threw open her front door. And there, on her doorstep, with his phone in one hand and the other raised in a fist as if to knock, was Arden.

Eight

Arden

"ARDEN?" RAVEN said in shock. Arden grinned.

"Forgotten what I look like already, Lightfoot?" he said. Raven shook her head.

"What are you doing here?" she asked. Arden took a step forward.

"Came to see you. Aren't you going to invite me in?"

"Sure, of course, but, why?" Raven took a step backward.

"It's our birthday. We always have our birthday together." Arden took another step forward. He was in the doorway now.

"Yes, but... but you're in West Bay." Raven stepped back, and found the edge of the kitchen counter.

"I was. But I couldn't see you on our birthday, and that was unacceptable. I thought to myself, what good is living another year if Raven isn't in it? So, I left the project early and drove into the city." He stepped forward. "And, wouldn't you know, as soon as I got here, I received a voicemail from you."

"You did?" Raven's voice came out small. Without taking his eyes from her, Arden pulled his jacket off and dumped it on the counter.

"Are you going somewhere, little bird?" he asked, eyeing her coat and boots.

"Um," she stuttered. "I was sort of... coming to see you." Arden slid an arm around her waist and lifted her suddenly onto the counter top. Her breath caught as she landed.

"To see me?" he asked, with an eyebrow raised. "Well, I'm here. So, you probably won't be needing this." He tugged her coat off and replaced it on its hook by the door, arms long enough that he didn't need to move from where he was standing.

"Now," Arden said. He closed the front door, then put a hand down on the counter on either side of her. With her sitting up on the bench, and him bent slightly at the waist and leaning on his hands, they were almost eye-to-eye. "Raven Lightfoot," he said, and brushed her chin with his thumb. "Have you changed your mind about us?" He touched the tip of his nose to hers, and the delicious, familiar scent of him overwhelmed her.

"Are you ready to come back to me now?"

Raven reached out and pulled in fists of Arden's soft t-shirt at his stomach. She looked into his big, yellow eyes, warm as summer.

"Yes," she said, and it sounded like the best word in the world.

"And you're sure this is what you want?" His breath was hot against her lips.

"This might be the only thing I've ever been sure about," she replied.

"Well, thank fuck for that," Arden said, and cupped one hand behind her head so he could pull her in and kiss her dizzy.

The lemonade fizz was uproarious.

***

One week later, Raven and Arden arrived in Cressock, and were enveloped in the embrace of their families. Riley had grown a foot in the last year, and Asher had just officially left school to work full time with Lachlan's company. Everyone had been supportive but not at all surprised when Raven and Arden announced their relationship over video chat a few days prior. Now, they were crammed around the Lightfoots' dining table, the six faeries as well as the Slivers.

"So, Arden, how are you adjusting to life in the city?" Nicholas asked, passing Annabelle a basket of rolls.

"You know, I was sceptical, for sure," Arden said. "But Raven's got such a good set-up. And Nola and Kofi have been super welcoming."

"He and Nola are already in cahoots," Raven added. "They call Kofi 'the human'."

"Ah he doesn't mind, he's a good guy," Arden said. Raven shoved him with her shoulder.

"You're lucky they let you move in on such short notice, you should be nicer."

Arden looked shocked.

"I'm delightful," he objected.

"And how was West Bay?" Cecelia asked him, while cutting her meat. "Did they finish okay without you?"

"Of course," Arden said. "They were more or less done anyway; they really don't need me that much."

"Are you staying with the project?"

"Yeah, we start up again in three weeks in a really run down town called Chilling."

"Oh, but you two just got together," Annabelle said, forlornly. She had very quickly become invested in the two of them as a couple – Nicholas told Raven when she got in that Annabelle and Cecelia had had a bet going about them ending up together since their birth.

"Ah but that's the best part," Raven said. "Chilling's only a

215

couple of hours out of Repanthe. Arden will be home on weekends."

Arden looked over at her, and smiled.

"Yeah. We'll be together all the time."

Raven smiled back.

"And you'll be back here for Yuletide?" Nicholas asked.

"Definitely," Raven assured him. "Wouldn't be anywhere else."

"Splendid!" Nicholas beamed. "Well, that's splendid." He tucked his napkin into his shirt, and his moustache danced as he chewed.

Sunday night, they rode the train back into Repanthe. The trip did not seem quite as long with the weight of Arden's head on her lap as he slept. They got home late, moved around quietly so as not to wake Nola and Kofi, and crawled into bed travel-weary.

Raven yawned, and Arden chuckled and pulled her into his arms.

"You have the most ridiculous yawn," he said. "It's such a big yawn for such a small faerie." Raven slid her knees in to overlap with his.

"Hey, I'm big," she said. Arden rolled over her, and caged her body with his.

"You're definitely not," he said, with a low growl.

"Well," she said, kissing his chin. "That's because it's night time and my spine is all compressed. I'll be bigger in the morning, you'll see. I just need some sleep."

Arden moved his lips in the hollow under her jaw.

"You want to sleep right now?"

"Yes," Raven said. "Big yawn, remember?"

"Hm." Arden touched his teeth just below her earlobe. "I

don't seem to recall."

He kissed her then, and, like every time, it brought her blood to bubbling over in an instant.

"You sure you can't stay up, just a little longer?"

Arden smoothed his hands up Raven's arms, pushing them to rest above her head. He pressed her hips down with his, and licked his tongue up her throat.

"You definitely want to go to sleep now?" he murmured in her ear.

"Well…" Raven struggled. "Maybe… not… *right* now."

Arden snickered.

"You want to stay up, a little bit, with me?" he said against her lips. Raven shifted under the weight of him.

"I could be convinced," she started to say, but Arden was already eating up her words.